Dear Romance R...

Welcome to a ... passion and
never-ending romance.

Welcome to *Precious Gem Romances*.

It is our pleasure to present *Precious Gem Romances*,
a wonderful new line of romance books by some of
America's best-loved authors. Let these thrilling his-
torical and contemporary romances sweep you away
to far-off times and places in stories that will dazzle
your senses and melt your heart.

Sparkling with joy, laughter, and love, each *Precious
Gem Romance* glows with all the passion and excitement you expect from the very best in romance. Offered at a great affordable price, these books are an
irresistible value—and an essential addition to your
romance collection. Tender love stories you will want
to read again and again, *Precious Gem Romances* are
books you will treasure forever.

Look for fabulous new *Precious Gem Romances* each
month—available only at Wal★Mart.

Kate Duffy
Editorial Director

ONE GOOD MAN

DEBRA WEBB

Zebra Books
Kensington Publishing Corp.
http://www.zebrabooks.com

ZEBRA BOOKS are published by

Kensington Publishing Corp.
850 Third Avenue
New York, NY 10022

First Printing: July, 2000
10 9 8 7 6 5 4 3 2 1

Printed in the United States of America

As always, special thanks to Hilary, a terrific editor.

This book is dedicated to my number one fan, Teresa Steele. Teresa is proof that dynamite does come in small packages.

ONE

"At ease, Sergeant."

Sergeant Jo Passerella released the breath she had been holding as she shifted to a more relaxed stance. Looking a two-star general in the eye without feeling somewhat intimidated always proved a bit difficult. Especially since he was someone new, whose reputation for unusual tactics had preceded him. Jo had heard Suddath war stories long before his actual arrival.

"Thank you, sir." Jo issued a smile despite the tension coiling in her stomach. This was her first appearance in the post commander's office, not to mention her first formal introduction to the new top brass of Fort McWayne. She wasn't in trouble—that much she knew for certain. The Army had a strict chain of command and her first sergeant had not informed her of any deficiencies in her performance of duty. Whatever the case, Jo couldn't prevent at least a little anxiety as she waited patiently for the general to begin.

Nope, she couldn't be in trouble, but that was

no guarantee that trouble wasn't waiting for her with the general's next words. Jo instinctively stiffened when General Suddath stood. The man's height alone would intimidate even her toughest male counterpart. She had heard the talk in the ranks. Fort McWayne would be this general's final military assignment. After retirement from his long and distinguished career as a military officer, his sights were set on the political arena as a second career.

The general released a long breath as he peered out the window behind his desk. Jo didn't have to look to know that two stories below troops marched and drill sergeants called cadence beneath the blistering Alabama sun. She almost smiled when she considered the patch adorning her left shirt pocket. She had worked hard to get this assignment, and she intended to be the best damned drill sergeant this post had ever seen. At only a little past five feet, and just over one hundred pounds, she'd had to work hard, period, at gaining recognition in "this man's" Army. But she had done it, and on her own at that.

"With increasing budget cuts each year," the general began, snapping Jo back to attention, mentally and physically. He turned to face her as he continued. "We find ourselves forever justifying our presence."

General Suddath shook his graying head. "Despite that annoying injustice, it is my belief that we should perform our assigned duties to the very best of our ability. Don't you agree, Sergeant?"

"Yes, sir."

"Community relations are a top-priority issue in today's Army. With that in mind, a desperate need has been brought to my attention." The general stepped closer. "A need we can fill, Sergeant."

Jo swallowed hard. "I'm sure we can, sir."

"I know we can, Sergeant." A knowing smile slid across his aristocratic features. "Are you familiar with Camp Serenity, a summer camp for troubled teens, located just outside Waynesville? There isn't another one like it in the entire state."

Jo frowned inwardly. Had she read something about such a camp in the post information packet she'd received before her arrival in Alabama? Nothing came to mind. "No, sir. Unfortunately, I haven't had the opportunity as of yet to take in much of the local culture. I spend most of my free time on the post."

General Suddath's smile broadened. "Well, Sergeant, you're going to see a lot more of the civilian community starting today."

A new kind of tension raced up Jo's spine. "Sir?"

"You've been assigned to support Camp Serenity as the physical training instructor for the next two weeks. And, if this special trial period proves successful—which I have no doubt that it will—you will be detailed to that assignment for the next six weeks."

Jo's heart dropped into her combat boots. "I'm not sure I understand, sir."

"What's to understand, Sergeant?" One thick, gray brow arched in challenge. "Do you have some sort of problem with your orders?"

Jo stiffened. "No, sir," she answered quickly, firmly, her words masking her inner conflict as she snapped back to attention.

"I'm counting on you, Sergeant," the general pressed. "This assignment is particularly close to my heart. As well as Mrs. Suddath's," he added with obvious affection. "She's an avid supporter of weight loss and physical training programs of all kinds. I can't tell you how much this trial run means to me, Sergeant Passerella."

"I understand, sir."

"Then fall out, Sergeant, your assignment begins immediately."

"Damn." Tom Caldwell blew out a disgusted breath, then ran his fingers through his hair to massage his aching skull. If he didn't get some help around here soon, he was going to be buried alive by paperwork. He glanced fleetingly at the empty corner by the door. This time last year Jack, his big old Labrador, had occupied that spot. Tom still missed his best friend. He couldn't remember a time in his life when he hadn't had a dog.

Tom shook the reminiscent feelings off as he shuffled the mountain of papers on his desk once more in an effort to find his final report. He knew he had done the report, he just couldn't find the blasted thing. Camp Serenity operated two four-week sessions each summer, with a two-week break in between. This summer's first session had been hell. The new physical training coach had quit mid-session. Though the man had left Tom in a tough spot, he harbored no hard feelings. Working with troubled teenagers was not an easy task, and if the new coach couldn't cut it, it was better that he left. But that ultimately dumped the work of PT planning and supervision in Tom's lap—along with too many other duties to mention. Case in point, the final report he knew he had written for the camp's first session but couldn't lay his hands on at the moment if his life depended upon it.

It happened every summer. And every summer, Tom swore he would figure out a way to keep it from happening the next year. Physical training coaches were harder to keep than wives. Not that Tom had ever had one. He'd never had time. Between teaching from mid-August to late May, then overseeing Camp Serenity, he had foregone a real social life for years now. But that hadn't seemed to bother him. At least not until recently. Lately he'd found himself wondering what life would be like if he found someone. Someone with whom to share his nights.

Another curse hissed past Tom's lips as he shoved that thought from his mind and considered the mass of papers before him once more.

"I've said it before and I'll say it again . . ."

There was a dramatic pause.

Tom looked up to find Reggie Travers, the camp's arts and crafts instructor, standing in the open doorway. Tom caught himself just before he groaned. He didn't have time for complaints this morning. And if Reggie were here, undoubtedly one would follow.

"What you need is a personal secretary," Reggie announced sagely as he removed his wide-brimmed Aussie-style hat and gingerly dusted away imaginary lint, then repositioned it on his balding head. "This office lacks organization and balance."

"I don't need a secretary, Reg." Tom dropped the handful of papers he'd started to rifle. "I need a coach so I'll have time to do *my* job." Tom gestured at the mass of papers on his desk. He forced a smile. If he didn't have another PT coach on staff before the next session began in just two short weeks—he didn't even want to think about that nightmare. But at some point he knew he would have to think about it.

"And what can I do for you this morning?" Tom offered in the most chipper tone he could manage. He knew that look. Reg had that screwy expression on his face. The one that spelled something between annoyance and outrage . . . and trouble for Tom.

Reg braced his hands at his waist and strutted across the room in typical Reggie fashion, pausing a few feet from Tom's desk. "The *ladies*—and I use the term loosely, I assure you—have only been here for two hours and already they're behaving worse than last session's hormone-overdosed adolescent bullies." He heaved an exaggerated sigh, one that involved a lengthy display of fascinating facial expressions. "I followed your orders precisely. First, I gave the group a nice welcome speech explaining all our rules and procedures, then I showed them around our facilities. But no one paid the least bit of attention to all my effort and hard work."

Tom rubbed at his right temple and fought the headache that threatened. He knew Reg would go on like this indefinitely if he didn't stop him. "What's the problem, Reg?"

"Well," Reg rolled his eyes dramatically. "Right off the bat no one liked their cabin assignments. This one didn't like that, and that one didn't like this. You know what I mean." Reg harrumphed. "They're worse than the kids." He lifted a skeptical eyebrow. "And that's saying something. Anyway, I worked the cabin assignments out to their satisfaction." He shook his head slowly, determinedly, from side to side, his gaze narrowed. "Then it started," he added grimly.

Tom stared at him blankly. "What started?" he prodded, in hopes of getting to the point of the conversation in this lifetime.

Reg leveled a somber gaze on Tom. "Harassment," he stated succinctly. "*Sexual* harassment."

Disbelief hit Tom like a sledgehammer between the eyes. Sexual harassment was not a phrase a youth camp director took lightly—even from Reg who had a reputation for theatrics and serious exaggeration.

"If this is a joke, Reg, it's not in the least bit funny."

"I beg your pardon," Reg retorted, obviously offended. "I would never joke about the subject." He lifted his chin defiantly, and iced Tom down with a glare. "I'll probably have bruises tomorrow."

Lines of confusion furrowed Tom's brow. "Bruises? Where?" he demanded.

Reg shrugged one shoulder. "I'd rather not go into the details, since we would likely both be embarrassed. It suffices to say that the behavior of these ladies is completely unacceptable."

The image of one of Fort McWayne's society matrons pinching Reg on the rear suddenly filled Tom's runaway imagination. He slapped a palm over his mouth, then rubbed his chin to prevent the grin from overtaking his lips. "Ah, Reg, I'm sorry, man, I'm sure—"

"All I want to know," Reg cut in pointedly, "is what you're going to do about it?"

Tom stood, opened his mouth to speak, then snapped it shut with a resigned shrug. How could he put this in a way that wouldn't offend Reg's somewhat delicate sensibilities? Yet Tom had to work this out. The new commander at the Army post had promised Tom a drill sergeant to act as Camp Serenity's PT coach for the next session. But Tom had to do the general a small personal favor

in return. Getting a core part of the camp's regular
staff to work through their break to support this
little request hadn't been a problem for Tom . . .
at least, not until now. Everybody knew how badly
he needed a PT coach.

Tom plowed his fingers through his hair again
and shifted. He glanced at Reg's indignant expression and decided there was nothing to do but do
it. He had sheltered him too long already. This
would be for his own good whether he knew it or
not.

"Reg, do you think the ladies' teasing has anything to do with that"—Tom gestured to Reg's attire—"that safari look?"

Appalled at the presumed non-compliment, Reg's
right hand flew to his heart as if he had been mor-
tally wounded. He looked down at himself, then
glared at Tom, his eyes widening in outrage. "And
just what, pray tell, is that supposed to mean?"

Tom glanced from Reg's indignant face to his
desk and back. Damn! He didn't have time for this.
"You know, man, you look like one of those guys
on the Discovery Channel who's about to embark
on an African safari." Tom bit the inside of his jaw
to keep a straight face and gestured again to Reg's
eye-catching clothing. "I mean, well, you have to
admit that between the khaki shorts and that
hat . . . maybe the ladies think you're . . . well,
you know . . . cute."

"Cute?" Reg crossed his arms over his khaki-clad
chest and surveyed Tom's worn T-shirt and sweat-

pants. Disapproval flickered in Reg's assessing gaze. "Is it my fault that I'm the only one around here with any sense of style?"

"I'm only saying—"

"Oh, I know exactly what you're saying," Reg countered hotly. "I agreed to stay on the next two weeks for what I thought was a good cause. You told me that the ladies participating in this little retreat were serious about wanting to lose weight and allow that beautiful, thinner, more fashion-savvy woman inside them to blossom."

God, had he really said that? Tom thought disgustedly. Yeah, he had. He'd been desperate. He needed Reg, just like he needed that new PT coach. If anyone could deal with obnoxious teenagers, a drill sergeant could. Hell, basic training instructors were some of the roughest, toughest soldiers in the Army. And if Tom were lucky and everything worked out, General Suddath might provide a coach next summer, too. Maybe even the summer after that. The man had hinted at that possibility. And it wasn't as if a U.S. Army drill sergeant could quit and go home.

"And that's what you'll do, Reg," Tom placated. He couldn't lose Reg now. "Mrs. Suddath and the other ladies will spend the next two weeks learning to eat right, to exercise, and to coordinate their makeup and wardrobes." Tom turned his palms upward in a helpless gesture. "And all that other stuff you know how to do so well. There's no way I can do this without you, Reg. Nobody knows more about presentation than you. Nobody."

Instantly Reg's ego perked up. He lifted one still-indignant eyebrow. "Talk to them," he demanded curtly. "For the purposes of their time here I'm their fashion consultant, not some boy toy," he added as he turned sharply and headed toward the door.

Well, that went over like a load of rocks. *Boy toy?* Tom shook his head then blew out a weary breath. "Reg . . ." Tom tried to humor him. He didn't want him to leave on a bad note. There was no point in both of them being miserable.

Reg paused at the door and turned back to Tom. "I'll leave the problem in your capable hands. Because I won't sacrifice taste for anyone's respect," he admonished with a flamboyant flick of his wrist.

"I promise I'll talk to them, Reg. You know I wouldn't do this if I weren't desperate," Tom reasoned. "We need a PT coach we can count on. When the general made this offer it came with the condition that we conduct this little retreat for his wife and a few of her friends. We have no choice. You know that, don't you? Besides, how bad can it be?"

Reg sighed dramatically. "I know," he relented reluctantly, then frowned. He looked Tom up and down again with clear disapproval. "You know, Tom, you really shouldn't wear gloomy gray." He made a tsking sound. "It washes out your complexion."

Tom glanced at his somewhat tattered, but comfortable attire, then back at Reg. They'd had this debate on Tom's fashion sense—or lack thereof—on numerous occasions since grade school. Not everyone had Reg's pizzazz. Tom swallowed the nasty retort that hovered on the tip of his tongue. He had known Reg too long to take real offense. Besides, he didn't dare tick Reg off any further. If Reg walked out on him, he would be in a hell of a fix. "Thanks, buddy, I'll remember that."

The sound of a vehicle skidding to a stop outside the office captured Reg's attention. "Oh, my," he said with feigned excitement, "it looks as if the calvary has finally arrived."

Hoping it was the drill sergeant he'd been promised, Tom quickly skirted his desk and hurried to the door. He could definitely deal with something going his way for a change. Today had been the pits, and tomorrow was looking even worse. A grin spread across his face at the site of the U.S. Army hummer, complete with a big, strapping soldier, parked in front of his office.

"Thank God," Tom muttered wearily, stepping onto the wide, wooden porch.

"Or Uncle Sam," Reg suggested from beside him.

Tom's grin, and hopes, faltered when the soldier gave a curt wave and drove away, leaving nothing but a thick cloud of dust behind him.

Reg's hand fluttered to his throat. "Gee, do you think it was us?"

Tom shot him a pointed glare, then stared after

the retreating vehicle. Just as a frustrated four-letter word blew past his lips, Tom noticed a silhouette forming as the dust settled. He squinted to make out the figure standing some twenty feet away.

The first word that came to mind when the dust cleared completely was *uniform*.

Then, *tiny*.

Staring right back at Tom stood a mite of a soldier whose duffel bag surely outweighed her by fifty pounds. And it was definitely a her, he decided after his second appraisal of elfin features. Even wearing that shapeless camouflage military getup, she was obviously female. Whether it was those slight, but still distinguishable, curves or that pretty face, Tom wasn't sure. He was only sure that it had to be a mistake.

She had to be a mistake.

In one smooth, seemingly effortless move, the woman pulled the heavy duffel onto her back and marched across the dirt road, up the steps, onto the porch and straight up to Tom and Reg.

"Mr. Caldwell?" she asked of Reg.

"Oh, no, sweetie," Reg said knowingly. "It's him you want." He gestured in Tom's direction.

After turning to Tom, the little soldier announced, "Sergeant Passerella reporting for duty, sir."

Any fleeting hope Tom had left withered and died on the spot. "There must be some mistake," he blurted before he could stop himself.

"Oops, time for me to go," Reg volunteered.

"Don't forget to speak to the new arrivals, *sir,*" he added before scurrying away.

Tom clenched his jaw against the directions he wanted to give Reg on just where he could go. He would settle with him later. Right now, Tom turned back to the half-pint soldier in front of him. He had to deal with her.

"Is there a problem, sir?"

"*You're* the drill sergeant General Suddath assigned to act as Camp Serenity's PT coach?" Tom asked lamely, and for lack of anything else to say.

"Yes, sir," she answered quickly. "I'll be organizing the physical training program for your youth camp, sir. With your approval, of course," she added efficiently. Too efficiently.

She was an absolute featherweight, Tom noted again, his gaze sweeping her petite frame. He was surprised that she even met the minimum weight requirements for military duty. And those deep brown eyes. He found himself staring into those wide, expressive depths. How could this beauty be a drill sergeant?

"It there something wrong, sir?"

Her question snapped Tom back to reality. This would never work. The boys, and some of the girls required to attend the program at Camp Serenity would outweigh this little soldier by seventy or eighty pounds. Not to mention that many would tower over her by several inches, if not a full foot.

Tom searched for the right words. Nothing came.

"I'm sorry, Sergeant Passerella, you're just not what I expected in the way of help."

Her expression remained neutral. "If you're concerned about my being able to handle myself, put your mind at ease, sir. I haven't met a woman or a man yet that I couldn't hold my own with," she explained, a subtle challenge in her tone. "I'm quite certain this assignment won't change my record."

"Some of these kids look like linebackers for the Green Bay Packers," Tom said just as pointedly. "In the last group we even had a couple who were more than a little violent. They had to be dragged away in handcuffs."

She didn't flinch. "I understand, sir." Her impatience showed through her considerable self-control. "I can assure you that I'm more than capable of handling myself in a tactical situation."

Tom frowned. "I'm not sure you do understand." He knew for sure he didn't. "What would you do, Sergeant Passerella, if six feet and nearly two hundred pounds of raging hormones were towering over you right now, threatening to do you bodily harm?"

Three seconds later Tom was lying flat on his back on the wooden floor with no air in his lungs. Her movements like lightning and seemingly effortless, Sergeant Passerella had knocked his feet right out from under him before he batted an eye.

"Good answer," Tom croaked.

Passerella extended a hand and helped him to

his feet. "Thank you, sir. I hope I didn't hurt you. I tried to go as easy on you as possible."

Easy? Tom tunneled his fingers through his mussed hair and manufactured a smile. "I'm fine," he managed to say past the humiliation clogging his throat.

"Good." Sergeant Passerella gave him a quick, but sincere professional smile. "When do I meet my troops, sir?" She shrugged lightly and color stained her cute little cheeks. "Trainees," she amended.

Still admiring the smile that did strange things to his insides, Tom forced himself to focus on her question. "The next group of kids won't arrive for two weeks," he told her distractedly. She had a hell of a smile for such a tiny thing.

A line of annoyance formed between those lovely eyes. "Two weeks?" she echoed.

"But we have a special session planned for the downtime," he explained. "We're conducting a trial weight loss and exercise program for Mrs. Suddath and eleven of her friends. It's a special favor for the general. I couldn't exactly turn him down," Tom added when her expression fell.

There was no mistaking the look on Sergeant Passerella's face then. The metamorphosis ran the gamut: disbelief, indignance, outrage. Her deep brown eyes kindled with the combined emotions.

"Are you saying, sir, that I've been pulled from my regular military duty—official duty—to assist you in the operation of a *fat farm?*"

Tom thought about that for a minute. Surely there was a more politically correct way of putting it. No, he supposed there wasn't. A smile teased his lips then. So, Tom mused, Sergeant Jo Passerella was just as surprised by her temporary assignment as he was by her tiny size.

He allowed himself a full grin. This was rich. The general had hoodwinked them both. "Consider it a service to your country, Sergeant Passerella," he suggested in a purposely patronizing tone. She looked daggers at him. "Of course, if you don't feel you can handle the assignment, I'm sure General Suddath can find a suitable replacement in no time at all."

Their gazes locked, and something distinctly adversarial but vaguely sexual passed between them, radiating undeniable heat. Tom felt a completely unprofessional stir.

"I can handle anything you throw my way, Mr. Caldwell," she countered evenly.

"In that case," Tom surrendered, "welcome aboard, Sergeant." He stuck out his hand. Slowly, warily, she accepted the offer. Tom's fingers wrapped around her much smaller ones. He shook her hand once, then quickly released it, but not before a surge of electricity jolted him. This was not a good sign. He shook off the feeling and nodded toward the group of cabins across the quadrangle. "You'll find Reg in cabin one orienting our new guests. He'll give you your cabin assignment and our official camp attire."

"Camp attire?"

"We're pretty relaxed around here, Sergeant, your uniform would be a distraction," he told her, complimenting himself for the quick thinking.

After a "yes, sir" and a snappy salute, one irate little sergeant strode out the door. Tom smiled. He couldn't wait to see if Miss Jo Passerella was as cocky without her battle fatigues, sergeant's stripes, and kick-ass combat boots. He had a feeling she would be.

Well, he considered, at least he had some help. He just hadn't expected it to come in such a tiny, feminine form.

Time would tell if dynamite really did come in small packages.

He already knew first-hand that she packed an undeniable charge.

TWO

"Miss . . . oh, Sergeant . . . Yoohoo, Jo!" a breathless, feminine voice trilled.

Exasperated, Jo stopped and turned to face the group of retreat guests she'd been assigned to whip into shape for the next two weeks. She groaned inwardly. *No,* she reminded herself. She would not consider this an impossibility—it was merely a challenge. She was a highly trained soldier. She could forego food and sleep, walk for days without stopping and hit a silhouette's upper mass three hundred meters away with a military-issue M16. Jo had the bolo badge to prove it. And a drill sergeant's patch to boot.

She could do this.

"Yes, ma'am," Jo acknowledged as Mrs. Suddath, the general's beloved—however hefty—wife, stumbled toward her. Think of it as a *challenge*, Jo reminded that part of her that wanted to doubt her ability to succeed in this mission. A Passerella never backed away from a challenge.

Mrs. Suddath fanned a tendril of salon-produced blond hair from her plump cheek with one crimson-nailed hand, then blew out a heavy breath. "Did you say we were going to walk two whole miles?" she asked warily. The southern belle smile on her ruby-red lips slipped a bit.

"That's affirmative, ma'am," Jo replied patiently. She positioned her arms behind her back and assumed an at-ease stance. As far as Jo could see, the only thing Mrs. Suddath had done regarding weight loss and physical training programs was avoid them like the plague.

Mrs. Suddath patted at the sweat dampening her flushed, cosmetics-embellished face. "Well, I'm just certain that we've walked that far already," she suggested in a honeyed tone that no doubt garnered her anything she wanted from the general. "Why, I've never broken a sweat like this in my entire life. I'm not sure it's healthy for a woman of my fragile nature."

Jo absently wondered how it was possible to bat false lashes quite so fast. She manufactured a smile for the general's wife. Mrs. Suddath was no doubt accustomed to acquiescence to her position as post commander's wife, if not her practiced charm. Jo had no intention of bowing to either. "We're almost halfway, ma'am," Jo countered firmly but respectfully.

"Halfway?" another middle-aged matron wailed as she plopped down on a nearby tree stump. "I don't think I can take another step."

Murmuring rumbled through the ten remaining stragglers as they stalled, then dropped to the ground, the nearest tree stump or large rock. Jo stifled the sigh of defeat that rose in her throat. No way in hell would a group of big, beautiful members of the officers' wives club cause her to fail in her assigned mission. She was a soldier. Failure was not an option.

"There's a marker at the one-mile point. We'll turn back there," she explained.

Nobody moved.

Jo moistened her lips and swallowed back the first words that raced to the tip of her tongue. These women weren't soldiers, and she had to tread lightly. She scanned the huffing, puffing clutch of couch potatoes and considered her options: Leave them, or motivate them into action.

Though the wayward thought was appealing, leaving them was out of the question.

Jo cleared her throat, and opted for another approach. "Well, I'm going to carry on. You ladies can catch up when you've rested suitably." Jo turned to take a step, but paused as if belatedly remembering some significant point she'd forgotten to mention. "Just one thing," she started slowly, "be sure to watch for lizards and snakes. They're everywhere in these woods," she warned before heading off down the trail.

It took about two seconds for the group to absorb the impact of her words. Jo smiled at the clamor of feminine shrieks and the shuffle of feet scrambling behind her. Nothing like a little extra motivation to shift goldbrickers into gear.

* * *

Tom had made a mistake.

One that he wouldn't soon forget. The image of Jo Passerella wearing well-fitting gray sweatpants and a white camp T-shirt was permanently tattooed across his memory. All the adult sizes were too large and Reg'd had to give her youth size. If Tom had left well enough alone, she would still be wearing her shapeless uniform.

But he'd had to go pushing the issue, and now he would pay the price. Tom had wanted the little sergeant to voluntarily go back to the post and have the general send him a big, burly soldier for the position at Camp Serenity. Losing her official military uniform and combat boots hadn't made her want to give up; nor had the dozen chattering ladies who were more interested in swapping recipes than listening to the PT coach's instructions.

Nope. By all indications, Miss Jo Passerella was here to stay. The half-pint obviously had a stubborn streak a mile wide. And, Tom admitted reluctantly, there was just something about all that determination that appealed to him on a very elemental level. Heat spiraled inside him, making him restless.

She was so tiny. A smile lifted one corner of his mouth as he considered that petite, yet gorgeous, little body. And those eyes—Tom almost groaned—a man could get lost in those chocolatey depths. It wasn't until he had seen her without her regulation cap that he noted her hair. Long, thick and shiny, neatly fashioned into a bun on her head. How he would love to see it tumbling over her proud shoulders. His imagination immediately conjured up the image of her naked with all that hair draping her slender body like a cape of dark silk.

Whoa, boy! Tom yanked himself from his forbidden fantasy. No way was he going there. Sergeant— Miss Passerella was his coworker, not to mention U.S. Government property. He was lucky to have someone, even a slip of a female, taking part of the load off his shoulders. He couldn't allow the adolescent impulses he was experiencing to screw this up. This was too important, way too important, for anything to get in the way.

Tom had to start thinking with his head, not his—

A loud call to attention interrupted Tom's intense mental conversation with himself. He strode to the door of his office just in time to see a half-dozen or so ladies sprawled flat on their backs in the dirt. The other handful of retreat participants were holding each other up in a half-sitting-half-lying-down heap. The whole crew looked as if they were at death's door.

"What the hell?" Tom muttered as he bounded off the porch and across the quad. He paused a good distance from the group to see how Jo would handle what appeared to be outright, exhausted mutiny. He didn't envy her the challenge of getting the ladies back on their feet.

"We'll need to do our cooldown exercises now, ladies," Jo instructed in her firmest military tone.

"You've got to be kidding," Beulah Jackson, the largest of the group, replied listlessly. "If Elvis

Presley himself stood right in front of me singing *Love Me Tender*, I couldn't do it."

"Cooldown is a crucial part of physical training," Jo asserted. Her hands were on her slim hips, her feet wide apart. Irritation made her pretty face tense. "It's not to be taken lightly."

"You're a harsh taskmaster, Sergeant Jo," Crystal Winton, the youngest, stated matter-of-factly as she struggled to her feet. She smoothed her brightly colored smock and surveyed her petered out companions. "All right, suck it up, girls, we have to listen to Sergeant Jo. This is for our own good."

Sandra Suddath was the next to get to her feet— by way of a redhead's shoulder for support. If Tom remembered the names and faces correctly, the redhead was the wife of General Suddath's aide-de-camp.

"Crystal's right," Sandra chided. "We're here to get in shape." She squared her sizable shoulders and faced the inevitable. "Go easy on us, Sergeant Jo. We're done in after that grueling workout you put us through."

Tom frowned. Grueling workout? The two-mile walk? He remembered clearly that the hike through the woods was the first item on the agenda. At the crack of dawn, Sergeant Efficient had provided him with a schedule of the day's planned physical training. Tom didn't know why, but he would prefer if Jo Passerella weren't quite so good at her job.

While he watched, Jo led the women through a very simple cooldown routine. If she had been any easier on them, they would have been napping. Despite his earlier affirmation, Tom found himself watching the slow, supple movements of her body. Bend and stretch. From her slender neck to her defined ribcage, her body screamed femininity. Her delicate size only stirred his protective instincts. He could imagine gliding his hand over each perfect inch of her toned body. Her skin would feel like satin, her hair like spun silk. And those lips. Tom moistened his own. Her lips were full, lush, and looked dewy soft. How would they taste? he wondered. Uniform or no, Jo was all woman and for the life of him, Tom couldn't put her out of his mind.

A raucous round of catcalls and whistles jerked Tom from his second forbidden fantasy of the day— and it wasn't even noon yet. Startled by his own reactions to Jo, Tom shook himself back to the here and now. The ladies called suggestive remarks and whistled as Reg strutted by. Tom couldn't believe his eyes or his ears. With his chin jutting out and his shoulders thrown back, Reg ignored the group entirely. But Tom knew with a certainty that he would hear all about it later.

Boy, would he hear about it.

"Good morning, ladies," Tom said, stepping forward and interrupting. He had promised Reg he would take care of this, and he would. Somehow.

Jo eyed Tom suspiciously as he approached, but the other ladies more than made up for her coldness. They gathered around him, patted his back and squeezed his arms, until they'd had their fill of hands-on greeting.

"I see you all know Reg, our fashion consultant," Tom announced the obvious.

Jo still watched him warily, as if fearing he might invade her territory.

"Just so you know, ladies, Reg has a very lovely wife named Cynthia at home."

A few jovial boos and hisses came from the now animated group who had apparently gotten their second wind. Maybe Reg should accompany them on their next scheduled physical activity.

"We'll try and do better at behaving ourselves, won't we, girls?" Sandra piped up, giving the vivacious group a conspiratorial wink. Sounds of agreement punctuated Mrs. Suddath's words.

"Thank you, ladies. I know he'll appreciate it." Tom glanced at his watch. "In fact, your first image transformation class begins in less than one hour." Tom smiled. "I'm sure you're all looking forward to *My True Colors* with Reg."

Their exhaustion totally forgotten, the lively ladies hurried, chattering and giggling, toward their respective cabins to prepare for their first session with Reg. Tom shook his head. What was it about guys like Reg that appealed so to the ladies? Was it his ability to bond so well with females or his extraordinary fashion sense? Tom looked down at his own not-in-vogue attire. Well, if that were the case, he was definitely a lost cause.

"I usually do my own dismissing."

Tom looked up to find Jo striding toward him, irritation in every step. She halted, toe to toe with him, and glared up. He opened his mouth to make a witty retort, but all rational thought evaporated when his gaze focused on the delicate freckles scattered across the bridge of her cute little nose. He had the sudden insane urge to kiss each and every one.

"These ladies are severely lacking in discipline and motivation. They don't need any additional distraction," she snapped. That dark chocolate gaze looked anything but sweet now. She was ready to do battle.

"Sorry about that, Jo," he offered humbly. Tom matched her hands-on-hips stance. "I'll try not to interfere with your orders next time."

She blinked, obviously taken aback by his use of her first name.

"You don't mind if I call you Jo, do you?"

"Of course not," she said quickly, taking a small, faltering step back.

Smiling inwardly, Tom advanced the step she had retreated. "Good. And you can call me Tom. We've never been very formal around here. In fact, I'd say we're pretty laid back most of the time."

"Fine," she said stiffly before backing up another little step.

That smile broke across his lips as Tom noted the uncertainty in those dark eyes. So G.I. Jo wasn't nearly as tough without her military gear. Just what he figured.

His smile faded. Or maybe she simply didn't like having her personal space invaded by anyone.

Or maybe it was specifically *him* she didn't like invading her space.

That ridiculous thought shouldn't have bothered Tom, but it did.

It seriously did.

"Do I look like a rabbit to you?" Mrs. Suddath demanded crossly. She glowered at her tray and the minuscule low-calorie salad it contained before directing her death-ray gaze back at the woman she was addressing.

A tall, thin, graying woman wearing an apron and a hairnet glared back at Sandra Suddath from across the lunch line. "No," the elderly cook snorted knowingly. "You don't look a thing like a rabbit to me." She squinted, looking Sandra up and down for several seconds. "In fact, I'd have to say you look more like a pi—"

"Is there a problem here, ladies?" Tom cut in smoothly. A charming smile slid across his lips.

Jo couldn't help but smile herself at his close save. She imagined that if the cook had finished her statement, Sandra Suddath would have scrambled over that lunch line and given her what for. Jo had already decided that Sandra's southern belle airs and graces didn't amount to much. She would bet her next month's pay that Sandra was a hellcat beneath all that Scarlett O'Hara refinement. Dear old General Suddath probably did the saluting at home.

Beulah Jackson and some of the other ladies continued to grumble about being unable to live on lettuce leaves, alfalfa sprouts and carrot sticks. Jo smiled at the vulnerability she recognized in the ladies' indignant complaints. They were really a good-natured bunch—except maybe for Sandra. Jo might not know from personal experience, but she realized how difficult it was to lose weight. And she had given them a pretty good workout that morning, considering they were not accustomed to strenuous physical activity at all. No doubt they were exhausted, and hungry for something more than a healthy, fiber-filled diet. But it was the only way to accomplish the mission.

Jo would never in a million years admit it, but succeeding in this assignment meant more to her now that she had gotten to know the ladies just a little. At first, she had simply been determined to perform her duty to the best of her ability. Now she wanted to make a difference with these women. Jo's own mother had been sedentary and overweight since Jo could remember. She had been too young and preoccupied with her education, and then her career, to take notice—until her mother had suffered a heart attack. Maybe Jo had a chance to help this bunch before something like that happened to one of them.

Geez, you're sounding like an episode from Sally Jesse, Jo mused.

"Won't you join me for lunch, Jo?"

Jo snapped out of her musings to find Tom Caldwell standing right in front of her. She jerked back a step. She wasn't normally easy to surprise. How had he sneaked up on her like that?

"Excuse me?"

"Lunch," Tom repeated. "I asked if you would join me for lunch."

Jo averted her gaze from his intense blue one. "Sure," she replied, though sure was far from how she felt at the moment. He made her nervous . . . or *something*. "I would be happy to, sir."

His smile was wide and boyish, and entirely too appealing. "Great. But don't call me sir. It makes me feel older than I care to admit."

Disturbed for reasons she didn't fully understand, Jo followed Tom through the lunch line. She hadn't really looked at him before. She had treated Tom Caldwell like she did the men in uniform. Jo gave them the respect that came with their rank—sometimes they deserved it, sometimes they didn't—but she never really looked at them as people. It was easier to maintain a professional relationship with other soldiers if you didn't get too close. Friendship got in the way of duty sometimes. So she didn't get too close and she didn't look. But something about Tom tugged at her.

Jo couldn't help herself now as she gazed at Tom. He was tall. Of course, most people were tall to her, but Tom was six feet or a little over. Thick blond hair, much in need of a cut, contrasted well with his tanned skin. He had an athlete's body, and a killer smile that excited her more than she wanted to acknowledge.

She absolutely refused to look into his eyes again. That particular characteristic of her new boss was far too distracting. His eyes were . . . amazing, to say the least. Jo had no intention of noticing them in the future. She would simply observe without seeing. She did it all the time. The next two weeks didn't need to be any different.

The cook—Hattie, according to her name tag— offered Jo a tray with a somewhat larger portion of salad. Jo accepted it with a smile. She wondered if the solemn-looking older woman was trying to tell her something. To most people, Jo looked as if she needed to eat more. But she was the proper weight for her height, and she intended to stay right there.

"So, have you gotten settled into your cabin?" Tom asked as he took the seat across the table from Jo. "Anything you need?"

"Yes, si—I have," she stammered. "The cabins are much nicer than I expected. I have everything I require."

Another of those broad, devilish smiles spread across his handsome face. Jo scowled. She didn't like being constantly reminded of how handsome he was.

"We receive a lot of private funding, which helps." He stabbed a cherry tomato and popped it into his mouth. "We could never have this many amenities if it weren't for the private donations."

"Where do the kids who attend your camp come from?" Jo had been curious about that since her arrival.

"The local schools mostly. If a kid has problems throughout the school year that aren't quite bad enough for legal measures, they're required to attend one summer session here before school resumes in fall. Most of the time it works," he added, pride radiating from those amazing blue eyes.

Jo silently chastised herself for looking into them after all. "What happens when the Camp Serenity program isn't effective?"

Tom blew out a heavy breath. "In those cases, we're required to report the behavior to the local juvenile authorities. As extreme as it sounds, it's the law, and our only real option."

"You don't agree with that?" Jo picked up on his hesitation right away.

Tom frowned, his fork halfway to his mouth. He set it aside and considered her question. "It's not that I don't agree with it—but it really is the last option and the only alternative. The parents are usually at their wit's end, and the school has already done all it can do. I just hate to see it come to that." He shrugged. "But it's better to do that, than risk those kids who don't shape up here becoming increasingly violent at school. Too many incidents like that these days."

The headlines from some recent tragedies across the nation flashed through Jo's mind. "True," she agreed. Despite her determination not to, Jo looked at Tom—truly looked at him. What made an intelligent, gorgeous guy like him spend his summer doing this kind of work? Did Camp Serenity pay especially well? She would bet not. It was probably practically volunteer work. A new kind of respect welled in Jo as she assessed the man before her. Beneath that blond hair, blue eyes and those devilish smiles was a man of unusual sensitivity. Someone who cared about social problems and the kids he was determined to help. Had she failed to give him credit where credit was due when they had first met?

Maybe.

Probably.

Tom Caldwell was a do-gooder, she decided. A do-gooder with a heart of gold.

Jo stiffened.

She'd always treasured her childhood memories of reading about knights in shining armor on big white horses, who rescued damsels in distress and kingdoms under siege. The kind little girls dreamed of when they read Cinderella and Sleeping Beauty. The kind of guy who made you fall in love with him when you were supposedly all grown up.

Jo resisted the urge to shake her head. She had a career. A career where spouses were a hindrance. If the United States Army wanted her to have a husband, they would have issued her one in basic training. No way was Jo falling in love with anyone. She would simply have to keep a safe distance from the man.

Tom smiled another of those killer smiles when he caught Jo staring at him. Her heart sank. He wasn't going to make this easy.

"So, tell me, Jo, what made a little bitty thing like you decide to join the Army?"

Annoyance rushed through Jo. This was the kind of patronizing attitude she'd battled her entire life. Maybe keeping her distance would be easier than she thought.

Maybe today's Army was looking for a few good men . . . but all she'd ever wanted was one. One good man. And Tom wasn't a contender.

Although judging by the stricken look on his face, he'd obviously just realized he had stuck his foot in his mouth. She wondered vaguely if he were accustomed to the taste of his own shoe leather. He seemed to put his foot in his mouth regularly. Or maybe he only did that when she was around. That notion gave her far too much pleasure.

"Nothing in particular," Jo said sweetly. "I just wanted to learn how to kick the crap out of big guys like you."

THREE

The next morning Jo paced back and forth before her sleepy-eyed trainees. She shook her head in disgust as Sandra yawned loudly, and Beulah started from the doze she had fallen into while standing in formation. Slackers, Jo fumed, the whole lot of them.

"Ladies, you will need to be in bed no later than 2100 hours in order to be prepared for the next day's activities," Jo said sternly. "You cannot perform well without proper rest. Rest is essential."

Sandra scowled and braced her hands on her ample hips. "Well, no one told us we had to be up at the crack of dawn," she groused.

"0600," Jo said as patiently as possible. "Six A.M. That's when we start our day here. If you had bothered to check the schedule posted outside the recreation center as instructed yesterday, you would have known that wake-up call was at 0530." Jo turned and paced determinedly in the other direction, her gaze moving from one groggy lady to the next. She resisted the urge to shake her head. "It

will be to your benefit, ladies, to stay informed
about your schedule."

Apologetic sounds and acknowledgments grumbled through the group.

"All right," Jo announced. "Let's get started."

Groaning and griping with every move, the
women began what could only be called a lethargic
warm-up. Jo struggled with her own disappointment, reminding herself that they were counting on
her to help them get in shape, whether they fully
realized it or not.

Jo hadn't seen Tom so far this morning. And, if
she were lucky, she wouldn't. He was too much of
a distraction, not only to her trainees, but to her as
well. Her brow creased into a frown. She had never
been so easily distracted before. How did he do it?
she wondered with growing irritation. He wasn't the
first good-looking man she'd had to work with in
close quarters. Nor was he the first do-gooder she'd
supported in a cause. It had to be something else.
But for the life of her, she couldn't figure out what.

"Push-ups, ladies," Jo ordered. "That means you
have to actually move your bodies off the ground."
She glared at the group sprawled in the dirt before
her. "Hands shoulder width apart, now push *up*."

Grunts and other sounds of enormous physical
exertion served as background music to the feeble
attempts at push-ups. Jo dropped and did five to
demonstrate. The women merely looked at her as
if she had lost her mind. But they tried, Jo had to
give them that. In fact, Crystal did a pretty fair push-

up, Jo noted. Maybe there was hope for this group after all.

Jo rolled her neck, then stretched her shoulders as she watched the women huff and puff. She hadn't worn her hair down in so long that it felt strange against her back. A long French braid held the thick stuff away from her face and out of her way. Jo didn't know what had possessed her to wear it in a different style today.

But it had nothing at all to do with Tom Caldwell.

Jo frowned when a military vehicle pulled through the gate on the other side of the quadrangle and braked to a stop. She squinted against the sun to see the soldier who got out. A package in hand, he strode directly up to Jo.

"Sergeant Passerella?" he inquired.

"That's right. What can I do for you, Private Tipps?"

He thrust the package in Jo's direction. "I have orders to deliver this package to Mrs. Suddath."

"Thank you, Private." Jo accepted the package. "I'll see that Mrs. Suddath gets it."

Private Tipps nodded, pivoted sharply and headed back to the hummer in which he had arrived. Jo watched the vehicle disappear through the gate.

Jo scanned the plain brown box she was holding. It had no markings other than Mrs. Suddath's name. With a shrug, Jo set the box aside and turned back to her trainees.

"On your feet, ladies."

Jo didn't miss the odd look that passed between Sandra Suddath and Beulah Jackson. Jo had the distinct impression that it had something to do with the newly delivered box. General's wife or no, the box would have to be inspected before delivery. Jo had a feeling that whatever it contained, it wasn't on Sandra's diet.

Forty-five minutes later, the entire group had completed the calisthenics Jo had planned for the morning workout. The sun was beating down and it was unusually hot for seven in the morning. A sheen of perspiration had dampened Jo's skin, due mainly to her having to demonstrate the various exercises repeatedly.

"Deep breaths, ladies," Jo instructed. "We're going to start the cooldown phase now."

Someone from the back row choked out a "thank God."

Jo illustrated each gentle exercise for the necessary cooldown, then walked around the group to see that each participant was properly executing the moves. Something in her peripheral vision caught her eye. Jo backed up a step and looked down at the box that had been delivered for Sandra. Jo frowned. A whitish liquid had leaked from the box and dampened the dirt around it.

Still frowning, Jo crouched next to the box and ripped the tape from the flaps. Behind her, a sudden hush fell over the panting group.

"Sergeant Jo, I believe that package is for me," Sandra Suddath said quickly.

"Yes, ma'am, it is," Jo returned, not looking up from the box she was opening. "But I'll need to inspect it first. There appears to be a problem."

"But . . . but . . ." Sandra sputtered.

Ice cream. The box held four half-gallon cartons of gourmet vanilla ice cream. Without pause or a second thought, her mouth set in a grim line, Jo picked up the box and walked to the Dumpster next to the nearby dining cabin. She didn't miss the simultaneous gasps of disbelief and horror from behind her when she tossed the contraband into the dumpster.

Dusting her hands off, Jo strode back to the formation. "Now," she said pointedly. "Form two lines, please. We have a long walk ahead of us."

"I didn't see that on the schedule, Sergeant Jo," Crystal Winton, probably the only one who had looked at the schedule, protested.

"That's another thing to remember, ladies," Jo said sweetly with a smile to match. "Always be prepared for the unexpected."

Jo stood alone in the darkness just outside the dining cabin that night. It was almost 2200 hours. Another hour and she would call it a night. She took a deep breath, enjoying the fresh, clean air. Though it was still muggy out, the dark sky was clear and a hint of a breeze stirred the leaves occasionally.

Jo leaned against a tree trunk and considered the strange fork in the road her life had taken. She almost laughed out loud as she considered that after six years of active duty, she was now standing in the middle of a youth camp temporarily turned into a weight-watchers' retreat. How had this happened?

Jo had worked so hard at being a professional soldier.

She heaved a disgusted sigh. Why had the general picked her for this assignment? Jo thought she had done a damned good job as a drill sergeant. Did the general somehow consider her the most expendable of his soldiers? Jo shook her head in denial. She knew she performed as well as any of the men. No one could make her believe otherwise.

Maybe she had been chosen because the initial mission involved the general's wife. Perhaps he felt Jo would understand Mrs. Suddath's needs better than a male physical training instructor.

That thought made Jo feel a little better.

Fabric rustled behind her. Standing stock still, Jo waited, her breath stalled in her lungs. Someone was coming up behind her. Adrenaline rushed through her body, producing telltale chill bumps on her skin. The sound came from right behind her now. Instinctively her right elbow slammed into a solid ribcage. A soft grunt broke the air. Jo whirled and kicked the feet from under her would-be assailant. A heavy body thumped to the ground. Moonlight spilled through the branches of the trees and revealed a tall man lying flat of his back.

Tom Caldwell.

Damn.

"Sorry, sir," Jo muttered as she helped Tom to his feet. "You shouldn't sneak up on a soldier like that. We react on instinct."

"I'll remember that, Jo," he assured her tightly as he dusted himself off.

Heat rose in Jo's cheeks as she considered that this was the second time she had swept Tom off his feet, literally. She hoped and prayed he wouldn't mention these incidents in his report for the general.

"I hope you're not hurt, sir," she offered meekly.

A line creased Tom's brow. "I thought we were past all that sir stuff," he reminded, clearly amused. "Tom," he reminded.

"Right." Jo nodded. "Habit, si—Tom."

Tom plowed his long tanned fingers through his disheveled hair. "Do you mind if I ask what you're doing out here at this time of night?" Genuine concern colored his tone.

Jo glanced from the dining cabin to the trainees' cabins thirty meters away, then back to Tom. "I wanted to make sure the ladies didn't raid the kitchen tonight." Jo squared her shoulders. "I informed you of this morning's contraband ice-cream delivery, didn't I?"

He smiled, and as usual, the sight played havoc with Jo's senses.

"Yeah, you did." He shot an amused glance at the darkened cabins. "But I don't think you have anything to worry about tonight. After today's workout, I'd say they've already given it up for the night."

"I just want to be sure," Jo countered, unconvinced of his assertion. "I've heard that the first forty-eight hours of a diet are the most difficult."

"So you're expecting more trouble?"

"Maybe. Probably."

"Come on, Jo, these gals are forty-five and older. Don't you think they're a little old for those kind of shenanigans?"

Jo let go a breath. Okay, maybe she was wrong. But she had a sneaking suspicion that something was going down tonight. Something that had Sandra Suddath's unique brand of ingenuity behind it.

"What are *you* doing out at this hour?" Jo asked suddenly, turning the tables on him.

Tom shrugged. "A habit, as you put it." He rubbed his side for emphasis.

"What kind of habit?" Jo persisted.

"I always walk the grounds before calling it a night," he told her. "Just to be sure that everything and everyone is secured."

"But these aren't kids, Tom," Jo threw back at him. "Surely you don't think these 'old' ladies would be up to anything?"

Tom blew out a breath of defeat. "Okay, point taken."

Jo grinned triumphantly. He really was a nice guy. Most men she knew would not have admitted defeat quite so easily.

"The truth is I like a nice stroll before bed," he continued. "Want to make the rounds with me, Jo? I doubt there's going to be undercover action around here tonight. Besides, everything in the kitchen is locked up tight, and only Hattie and I have a key."

Jo's grin left her lips. She was still mulling over the image his words evoked. The thought of Tom

ONE GOOD MAN   49

Caldwell in bed, naked save for a tangled sheet, flashed before her eyes. She blinked it away. "Well, I—"

"Come on, Jo," Tom urged, tugging her by the arm as he moved from under the tree. "I don't bite."

Reluctantly, Jo followed. She didn't want to spend time with him alone—especially in the dark. Normally she would have said no and gone her own way. But she hadn't this time. Why was that? Jo clasped her hands behind her back and tried to rationalize her recent behavior. The full moon suddenly caught her attention. Relief filled her. People often acted out of character during a full moon . . . or so it was said. That had to be the reason she was feeling out of sorts tonight.

"Do you have family, Jo?" Tom gave her a quick sideways glance, then stuffed his hands into the pockets of his shorts and directed that analyzing gaze dead ahead.

"Four older brothers," Jo responded proudly, forcing a calm she didn't feel. "Two in the air force, one in the navy and one in the army like me. And my father is a retired military man himself."

Tom nodded sagely. "That would explain a lot," he said quietly.

Jo's step slowed. "What are you suggesting?"

His shrug was slight, the barest lifting of one wide shoulder. "I'm only saying that you had to get tough with four older brothers in the house."

Jo bit her lower lip to hold back the smile, then murmured, "You think I'm tough?"

Tom chuckled good-naturedly. "Let's just say that actions speak louder than words."

Feeling suddenly brave, Jo went for broke. "So you've decided you don't want to send me back for a bigger and better model?"

Tom hesitated, using the moment to capture her gaze. Those blue eyes twinkled with what might be amusement . . . or something like it. Anticipation surged through Jo's veins. Of what she didn't know, and she definitely didn't want to analyze it.

"Nope, I think I'll keep you."

A strange, heat-filled moment passed. Before Jo could decipher the look in Tom's eyes, he turned and started forward again. Feeling as light-headed as she did bewildered, Jo followed.

They walked without talking for a while. Jo wondered if he were struggling with what had just passed between them. Or had he even felt it? Frowning, Jo mentally scolded herself. She wasn't some silly schoolgirl. She was twenty-four years old, and a professional soldier in the United States Army. She knew better than to behave in such an adolescent manner.

What on earth was wrong with her?

"I'm the oldest in my family," Tom said, breaking the awkward silence that had seemed to stretch forever.

"Brothers or sisters?"

"Two sisters and one brother." He smiled. "One doctor, one lawyer, and one aerospace engineer."

Jo wondered briefly if Tom's siblings looked like him. All the Passerellas had dark hair and eyes. All were tall and large-framed, except Jo. She was the runt of the litter. She smiled. And Tom was right, her older brothers had made her tough. Tough enough to fend for herself during those turbulent teenage dating years; and definitely tough enough to handle herself now, in or out of uniform. Well, physically anyway.

Another of those rare breezes stirred the sultry night air. Jo lifted her face to the cool breath of nature. It was a beautiful evening. Even if she were probably making a mistake by lingering in this man's company longer than necessary.

Jo stole a glance at Tom's strong profile.

A big mistake. And there was no probably about it.

"What made you decide to become a teacher?" she found herself asking. Teaching didn't seem nearly as exciting as the careers his siblings had chosen.

"The kids," he responded without hesitation. "From the time I was fifteen I worked in one youth program or another." He gave another slight shrug. "I guess you could say that it's my calling."

"No kids of your own?" Jo could have bitten her tongue off. Why in hell had she asked that?

Tom shook his head. "Nope. No wife, either."

Jo was thankful the moon was blocked by a thick stand of tall trees at the moment. Her face burned with humiliation. His marital status or number of dependents wasn't supposed to matter to her.

"How about you, Jo? Ever been down the aisle?"

She could feel his gaze on her, so Jo kept hers focused straight ahead. The moon drenched them in its silvery glow once more as they cleared the stand of trees. "Only as a bridesmaid," she told him succinctly. "Remaining single is simpler in my chosen career." It was Jo's turn to shrug now. "Besides, I don't have time for real romance."

"Isn't that the truth," Tom murmured.

Silence settled over them as they covered the final stretch of camp property, bringing them full circle and back to the dining cabin.

"Do you ever get lonely, Jo?"

The question stopped Jo dead in her tracks and she stared at him despite her desire to avoid eye contact. "What?" she asked more sharply than she had intended.

"Do you ever feel like you're missing something?" He seemed at a loss for words for a second or two. "You know, like you're missing something that should matter because you're so absorbed in your work. Too focused on everything but yourself."

Jo opened her mouth to state an unconditional no, but a new emotion in his gaze stopped her. Wonder . . . confusion, maybe. The same things she herself had felt recently—very recently, in fact. Starting with the moment she laid eyes on *him*.

"I don't know," he added slowly. "Something that you might wish for the rest of your life you hadn't let slip away." His words were nothing more than a silky whisper on the breeze.

There was no mistaking the desire in his eyes now, or her own powerful response. Slowly, as if time had almost stopped, his hand came up to her face. Jo closed her eyes as his fingertips traced the outline of her jaw. Sensations exploded inside her, making her heart slam against her ribcage. She ordered herself to back away, but her body refused to obey the command—her control went utterly AWOL.

Jo's breath caught when she felt the whisper of Tom's warm breath against her lips. He was going to kiss her. The heart thundering in her chest suddenly stilled, and Jo melted with the heat spiraling wildly inside her.

The sound of glass breaking shattered the spell. Jo jerked back a step. So did Tom. Instinctively, she surveyed the darkness around them. A beam of light flashed across a window in the rear portion of the dining cabin. Metal clattered.

"Someone's in the kitchen," Tom said, already headed toward the dining cabin's entrance.

Jo double-timed it to the steps. They took their time climbing the wooden steps and crossing the porch. One squeaky board could give them away.

She had known this would happen. Jo had a gut feeling all evening that something was up. Tom might be surprised, but she certainly wasn't.

Slowly, quietly, Jo and Tom made their way across the dark dining room and to the double doors that entered the kitchen. Tom leaned close and whispered in Jo's ear. She shivered in spite of herself.

"On the count of three we'll swing the doors inward and flip on the light. The switch is on my side."

Jo nodded her agreement, knowing that his face was close enough for him to feel her action. She shivered again. He sighed. Oh, no. How had she let this happen?

She had left her post and allowed herself to become distracted—no, involved—with a man who was technically her superior.

Tom paused in his murmured countdown as disembodied voices drifted through the closed doors.

"Oh, my God, this is good. Hmmmm . . . mmmmm."

Jo recognized Sandra Suddath's voice immediately.

"Wow, it's like sex," the woman moaned loudly. "Only better," she added wickedly.

Giggles rippled through the group, which probably consisted of at least four, Jo decided.

"Hurry, Sandra!" Beulah ordered sharply. "Pass it down this way."

"Patience, Beulah," Sandra said between more enthusiastic sounds of pleasure. "Rank does have its privileges, after all."

Beulah grumbled some retort Jo couldn't make out.

"Now, Hattie," Sandra said, then obviously paused to take another bite and moan loudly. "You must realize that you left me no alternative, dear."

A strained, muffled sound echoed next. Jo

frowned, her concern growing. It sounded almost as if someone were trying to speak through a gag.

"Just remember, Hattie, old friend," Sandra added knowingly. "Never, ever get between a fat girl and her next proper meal."

More giggling.

"Three," Tom growled in a stage whisper—his exhausted patience audible.

Jo and Tom shoved the doors inward and two seconds later bright light filled the large kitchen.

Jo's mouth dropped open and her eyes rounded in disbelief as she stared at the scene before her. Sandra, Beulah, the redhead named Mildred, and Veronica—always the quiet one—were perched on a long stainless-steel table eating chocolate ice cream from the carton. Each plump, rosy face was frozen, eyes round with realization that they had just been caught. Poor Hattie was sitting in a chair, bound and gagged.

Jo flicked a glance at Tom, who looked every bit as flabbergasted as she.

"Oops," Sandra said sweetly, the first to recover. "Looks like we're busted, girls."

Jo stiffened her spine and glared a warning at the general's wife. "Ladies," Jo announced brusquely. "You will return to your quarters at once. And I will deal with you at 0600 hours."

The four hopped off the table and scurried toward the door. Tom was busy freeing poor Hattie.

Veronica paused before following her partners in crime out the door. "Sergeant Jo, are we in really big trouble?" she asked meekly.

Jo gave the woman her best drill sergeant's glare, and Veronica wilted. "Let's just say that you're definitely going to regret this."

FOUR

Jo heaved a sigh of satisfaction as she strode toward the showers shortly after dinner the next evening. She had accomplished a great deal today. Sandra, Mildred, and the other two from last night's clandestine party had worked kitchen detail all day. Every square inch of the dining room and kitchen had been thoroughly scrubbed and all the stainless steel polished. Hattie had ruled over the undertaking with an iron fist.

Jo couldn't prevent the little smile that surfaced at the memory of Sandra's haggard expression as the woman trudged toward her own cabin thirty minutes or so earlier. Today would certainly go a long way in teaching the headstrong southern belle a lesson in self-discipline, teamwork and, Jo hoped, humility.

The rest of the group had participated in swimming and canoeing, as well as an informative class on poise and posture from Reg. Jo's smile widened at the thought of Reg. He really was a nice guy, and he knew everything about "presentation." The retreat participants weren't the only ones listening when Reggie Travers talked. With only older brothers, Jo had learned virtually nothing about social grace. She might as well make the most of her time at Camp Serenity, she resolved. Who knew when coordinating colors and accessories might come in handy?

And it had nothing at all to do with Tom Caldwell.

Jo chewed her lower lip, her step faltering. Why was Tom her first thought every time anything remotely feminine crossed her mind? She had absolutely no intention of trying to woo him or any other man at this point in her life. She was young, she had plenty of time for romance . . . later. Jo cringed inwardly when last night's near kiss flitted through her mind. Heat rushed through her so fast it made her dizzy. How had she let that happen?

She knew better.

Jo sighed mightily. Knowing better and doing better were two different things. That's what her father would say, and the full meaning of it hit her squarely between the eyes last night. She knew better.

And she would definitely do better.

Definitely.

A sound caught Jo's attention. Frowning, she stopped, then turned slowly toward the rustling in the nearby bushes. She listened intently, analyzing all she heard. Her first thought was that an animal would scurry out of its hiding place at any moment.

But a muffled curse, distinctly male, obliterated that possibility.

"Who's there?" Jo demanded in her sternest military tone. She readied for defending herself.

"Jo?" Tom Caldwell replied hesitantly from the thick bramble of greenery.

Jo's frown deepened. "What are you doing in the bushes?" she asked crossly as she edged a step closer. She willed her heart rate to slow. The fact that its rapid beat had more to do with the sound of his voice than her being startled annoyed the fire out of her.

"I have a small problem," he replied in a desperate whisper.

Jo moved another step closer. "What kind of problem—exactly?" she ventured. Her own hesitance echoed loudly in her tone.

Abruptly, one long-fingered hand snaked out and grabbed Jo's arm. Tom yanked her into the bushes to join him without explanation. Instinct battled with the renewed heat his touch sent roaring through her.

"This sort of problem," he murmured heatedly.

Jo blinked, breaking the strange hold his gaze always had on hers. She blinked again, then stared in outright shock at Tom's state of . . . undress. With his free hand, he held one bushy branch over his . . . his . . .

"Someone stole my clothes," he growled impatiently. "I need you to go to my cabin and bring me back something to wear before anyone else comes along."

Bewildered, and damned befuddled, Jo made herself look only at his eyes. "What were you doing with your clothes off?" There had to be an explanation. A grown man didn't run around—even in the bushes—buck naked. At least not a responsible man like Tom.

"The main supply line to the men's showers sprang a leak and the plumber can't come until tomorrow. I decided to take a dip in the lake since I couldn't shower." Irritation furrowed his wide brow. "Someone obviously saw me and decided to play a little prank." He released Jo and plowed his fingers through his wet, disheveled hair. "If I find out it was Reg, I swear I'm going to kill him."

A grin curled Jo's lips. "Don't do that," she protested quickly. "He's far too valuable to the success of this, uh, mission."

"Right," Tom groused, as if remembering how the ladies loved Reg. Tom let out a disgusted sigh. "I'll kill him in two weeks."

The grin on Jo's lips slipped a notch when her wandering eyes took in Tom's utterly masculine body. Wide, wide shoulders. Well-defined, muscular chest and arms. A flat, taut abdomen. Long, muscled legs. Her breath evaporated in her lungs when her mesmerized gaze roved back up to the sprinkling of golden hair on that perfect, sculpted chest. He was absolutely gorgeous . . . amazing . . . and completely naked.

Jo swallowed.

And she was staring.

She blinked again. "Clothes," she managed hoarsely. "You need clothes."

"That would be nice," he said stiffly.

Jo backed up a step. "I'll just . . . ah . . . go get them." She looked anywhere but at him. Why did she have to be the one to walk by in his time of need?

"Hurry, Jo," he urged. "Before someone else—"

At the precise instant the branch slipped from his grasp and Jo got a full frontal view of Tom Caldwell in the buff.

She stood, rooted to the spot, gaping for a good five seconds. Then, without looking back, she ran like hell toward the man's cabin.

Tom was very, very wrong, Jo realized as she skidded to a halt at the steps to his door. He didn't have a small problem at all. She licked her suddenly dry lips. He had a rather large problem, in fact.

And now that she had seen it, it was her problem too.

"So this often happens when the kids are around?" Jo asked slowly and from outside Tom's hiding place.

Feeling like a complete idiot, Tom quickly pulled on the sweats Jo had just handed him through the bushes. She hadn't brought underwear, and he wasn't about to ask her to go back for them.

"Yeah," he said, as he yanked the T-shirt over his head. "The kids do it to each other all the time."

Hopping on one foot, Tom pulled on and tied first one sneaker and then the other. "They even did it to Reg once." Tom smiled at the memory. Reg had been fit to be tied. A couple of girls had discovered that Reg liked an occasional midnight dip. Reg, a cluster of leaves held over private areas front and back, had stormed into Tom's cabin that night. He had been so irate and determined to ensure that Tom found the culprits that he hadn't even taken the time to put on any clothes first.

"Reg?" Jo said incredulously. "I'll bet that didn't go over so well."

Straightening, Tom combed his fingers through his mussed, still damp hair. "Nope."

Tom stepped out of the bushes, purposely avoiding eye contact with his little rescuer. He hadn't missed the way her mouth dropped open or that shocked expression that had captured her pretty face when the branch slipped from his grasp. The fact that he had been semi-aroused simply by her presence hadn't helped any. His male ego worried with the notion that she had either been pleased at what she had seen or horrified. Tom frowned. He had to stop thinking about sex in connection with Jo Passerella.

"Reg wasn't pleased with the way I handled the girls' punishment either," Tom explained further, forcing his thoughts back to her question rather than the tense moment that had passed between them.

Jo shifted awkwardly, her gaze anywhere but on

Tom. She was clearly as uncomfortable as he was. "That's why you think he did this?"

"Yeah. He was probably just passing by and took the opportunity to settle an old score." Tom suddenly noticed the towel and bottle of something resembling shampoo Jo clutched under one arm. She had been headed for the shower. His mouth went dry at the image that abruptly came to mind. Jo naked, water sluicing over her satiny skin. Her silky hair wet and hanging down her back like dark falling water. His gut twisted with need, and desire weighed heavy in his loins. Tom blinked, then gave himself a swift mental kick. What the hell was wrong with him? He'd lost his mind, that was the problem.

"Maybe we should do cabin checks," he suggested. Focus, Tom, old boy. Now was the time to focus on the business at hand—running this damned little retreat, not having your way with your newest PT coach.

Jo looked him straight in the eye then. "You sound somewhat less convinced that those sweet southern belles are too old for shenanigans." A smile teased her full lips, making Tom's heart, as well as other parts of his anatomy, react.

"After last night, I wouldn't put anything past them." He glanced at her towel again. "If you're headed for the showers I can do the cabin checks myself," he offered, though he hoped she would accompany him.

Jo shrugged. "I can hit the showers afterward."

Tom nodded and started forward. *And maybe*

you'll ask me to join you. He thrust his hands into the pockets of his sweats and forced that wicked, though appealing, idea from his mind. He wasn't being fair to Jo. She was here to teach these women how to get in shape, not assuage his personal needs. Tom licked his hungry lips. Hell, he had hardly noticed his needs in too long to remember until she came along. He frowned. What was it about this woman that tempted him so. He swallowed. Damned if he wouldn't give most anything to find out.

Sandra and the usual suspects that hung out with her—Mildred, Beulah, and Veronica—appeared to be engrossed in a game of Go Fish in their cabin. The rest of the ladies were watching a video in the recreation center. Reg was reading in the dining room while Hattie was finishing up for the night. The two usually played a game or two of Rook before going to their respective cabins. Reg swore he knew nothing about what had happened to Tom's clothes. And Tom knew the man well enough to know that he was telling the truth. That meant the culprit had to be one or more of the ladies.

Despite the pilfering of his attire, all appeared to be in order, but Tom had a nagging hunch that nothing was as it seemed.

"There's no need for you to walk me to the showers," Jo argued when she turned to go, and Tom followed. "I can take care of myself."

Tom had no doubt that Jo could take care of herself, but he just wasn't ready to part company

with her yet. "I don't mind," he countered non-
chalantly. "Like I told you, I take a walk every
night anyway. I might as well get a head start on
it now."

Frustrated with his persistence, Jo relented and
headed for the showers. The image of Tom naked
and aroused kept playing in vivid color across the
private theater of her mind. How was she supposed to put *that* picture out of her head? She
moistened her lips. The man was gloriously male.
Sinfully sculpted in hard muscle and tanned skin.
Heat pooled at her center when she considered
how it would feel to touch that golden skin. To
glide her palms over that muscled terrain. To taste
those full, sensuous lips. Desire barbed through
her, making her moist where she was already too
warm.

Jo took a long, slow breath and forced her heart-
beat to return to normal. She stole a glance at the
man beside her as they neared their destination. He
seemed as tense as she. Jo's brows drew together in
a frown. She supposed that having had his clothes
stolen, then being exposed to a total stranger would
leave him feeling a bit out of sorts. If Jo felt awkward, how must he feel?

Disconcerted, Jo paused outside the door leading into the women's shower facility. The bright
light of the moon was mostly blocked by the trees,
but a dim glow spilled from the open doorway,
casting Tom's handsome features in becoming
shadow.

"I . . . I want you to know that what happened

this evening was no big deal," she said carefully, forcing herself to make eye contact. She hoped the light was low enough that he couldn't see the heat of remembered embarrassment rising in her cheeks.

His gaze darted side to side before locking with hers once more. "Okay," he said just as carefully, as if he wasn't quite sure what she meant.

Jo swallowed to clear her throat. "I mean, as a soldier I've seen plenty of naked men."

Tom nodded once. A mixture of confusion and amusement lit up those amazing blue eyes. "That's good to know," he replied politely, but the grin overtaking his lips belied his tone.

Jo's choice of words echoed in her ears. Her cheeks flamed red-hot now. "That's not what I mean . . . I mean," she stammered. "It was . . . it was no big deal."

His growing amusement more than evident now, Tom opened his mouth two full seconds before he spoke. "Oo . . . kay," he said, drawing out the one word.

Jo shook her head in self-disgust. "I don't mean that either. I mean—"

Two long fingers pressed lightly against her lips. "I know what you mean," he said softly, all signs of amusement gone now.

Fire zipped from her lips straight to her breasts, making them tingle. Desire struck Jo low and hard in her belly, rendering her self-control totally inoperative. Her towel and shampoo fell unnoticed to the ground. Those perfect artist's fingers traced her jaw, then slid lower to curl around her neck. His gaze holding hers captive, Tom pulled her closer, then leaned down to align his mouth with hers. Jo's breath caught in expectation of his kiss. She prayed he wouldn't be interrupted this time. His warm breath whispered across her lips.

"I'm going to kiss you, Jo," he murmured before allowing the first, gentle brush of his lips. Tom cupped her face with both hands, paused two beats to give her time to protest, then settled his mouth firmly over hers, making good on his warning.

Too many sensations to name bubbled up within her.

She knew she should stop this. It wasn't right. She knew better. But the feel of his lips against hers, his hands caressing her face so tenderly—she just couldn't bring anything that felt this wonderful to an end. She wanted more.

Hesitantly, her eyes squeezed tightly shut, she allowed herself to respond. Her palms molded to his broad chest. The feel of heat and rock-hard muscle made her quiver inside. His now familiar male scent filled her lungs. Jo's fingers fisted in the soft cotton of his T-shirt, drawing him closer. She wanted to feel his body against hers, to saturate her senses with Tom Caldwell.

His tongue traced the seam of her lips and Jo's pulse raced. Tentatively, she opened for him. Tom filled her with his taste, hot and excited. A sound, her moan of approval, echoed between them. Her heart pounded with the dizzying emotions raging through her veins. Somehow his hands found their way to her hips. Tom lifted her against his full erection. Jo moaned again. She felt her body moisten in anticipation.

Tom stilled.

His taunting mouth drew away from hers ever so slightly, but the feel of his uneven breath against her ultra-sensitive lips sent renewed desire rushing through her. Jo's own breathing was ragged. She needed more. She wanted more. But he had stopped. She held on tightly and braced herself against the cry of desperate protest that swelled in her throat.

He pressed his forehead to hers and let go a mighty breath. "How am I supposed to just walk away after that?" he rasped, his voice thick with desire. Those magic fingers of his found their way back to the pounding pulse point at the base of her throat.

Jo chewed her lower lip until it hurt, the pain jerking her back to reality. "We shouldn't have done that." She swallowed. "It was a mistake."

He tensed. Jo felt the almost imperceptible change even before he straightened, moving slightly away from her.

"Look at me, Jo," he commanded, his voice still soft despite the tension now radiating from him.

Slowly, Jo opened her eyes and looked up at him. His gaze was as uncertain as hers surely was.

"Now tell me it was a mistake."

Jo swallowed. She ordered her fingers to relax their hold on his shirt and dropped her arms to her side. Reality hit her like a tidal wave. She flinched. "It was a mistake," she forced herself to say, though her words lacked the conviction she knew she should feel. "In the army we would call it—"

"I know what you would call it," he said sharply.

Jo blinked at his curt reply. "I'm sorry," she offered. She was a highly trained soldier. Jo had spent years training to react on instinct, not emotion. This shouldn't have happened. It was her fault.

Tom plowed his fingers through his hair and released a shaky breath. He shook his head slowly from side to side. "No, I'm the one who's sorry. I was out of line." A halfhearted smile lifted the corners of his mouth. "It won't happen again."

He looked so sincere, yet so confused. Jo ached to put everything else aside and learn the pleasures of knowing this man fully. She produced a weak smile of her own, and pushed away the emotions she knew she should not feel. "Right. We're adults. We can handle the situation."

He nodded his agreement. "Well, I'll just say good night, then." Tom backed up a step.

"Good night," Jo managed.

Both remembered the towel and shampoo on the ground at precisely the same instant and reached for them. Their fingers tangled on the terry cloth. They stood up simultaneously. Whether Tom was aware of it or not, his blue eyes gave away all that was on his mind as he relinquished his hold on the towel. He wanted her, Jo realized, just as much as she wanted him.

He gave her another of those almost-smiles, turned and disappeared into the darkness. Jo closed her eyes and released a long breath. *Okay,* she told herself, *get a grip.* She was on assignment here, not personal leave. She had orders—orders straight from the general himself. She could not fail under any circumstances. Nothing was going to get in her way.

Not even Tom.

Summoning her resolve, Jo grabbed her bottle of shampoo and strode purposefully into the shower facility. Tom was a nice guy and she liked him. But he couldn't add another stripe to her sleeve. He couldn't influence her future in the military. General Suddath could. No way could Jo risk screwing up on this assignment.

Slowing as her surroundings once more came to the forefront of her awareness, Jo frowned. The facility had twelve shower stalls, six on each side. All but the one on the right at the far end were marked out of order. How could that be? They were all working last night. Then Jo remembered Tom saying something about the plumbing being on the fritz. Maybe the women's showers were affected as well as the men's.

Jo placed her towel on the wooden bench outside the stall. She twisted both knobs on the faucet open all the way. Experience had taught her that it took some time to get the hot water going, if there was any left. While the spray blasted against the old, utilitarian tile, Jo toed off her running shoes. She rolled off her socks and tucked them inside her shoes. The Camp Serenity T-shirt went next, then the sweatpants. Jo folded her clothes and stacked them in a neat pile on the bench. She removed her bra and panties next, adding them to the growing pile.

After adjusting the water to a bearable but still plenty-hot temperature, Jo stepped into the shower. She closed her eyes for a long moment and allowed the heat and steam to relax her tense muscles. Her eyes still closed, with the hot spray aimed directly on her neck and shoulders, Jo took her time undoing her long braid. Despite her best efforts she found herself imagining how it would feel to burrow her fingers into Tom's thick blond hair, and have him respond in kind. A smile slid across her lips as she considered how he had tasted. He had obviously drunk flavored coffee just before his little dip and had tasted pleasantly of French vanilla. And he had tasted hot, very hot. She had felt his eagerness, his need.

Jo threaded her fingers through her hair and massaged her scalp as she tilted her head back beneath the spray. Her breasts tingled when she recalled the memory of how Tom's body had felt against hers. He had been hard for her. Jo's nipples reacted. He hadn't touched her breasts. How would it have felt, she wondered, to have his hand close firmly around her breast? To have his fingers roll and pinch her tightly budded nipple? To have his mouth close over that aching part of her and suck . . . hard.

Tension coiled inside Jo as she conjured Tom's

naked image to mind. How would it feel to have that much powerful masculinity pressing down on her? To have him—all of him—inside her?

Jo's eyes popped open. She blinked, twice. She couldn't think like that. She could not have an affair with Tom Caldwell. The kiss was a mistake. These fantasies were a mistake.

She had to stop thinking about him as anything other than her superior. This assignment would be over in a few weeks and she would be going back to the post. Tom would go back to the high school where he taught. They would likely never see each other again.

Jo swallowed tightly. There was something about that last thought that didn't sit well with her. But it was the truth. Jo had always been honest with herself. She wasn't about to change now. The feelings she and Tom were experiencing were nothing more than sexual chemistry. Lust. They had nothing in common, and certainly had no future together.

And since Jo didn't do casual affairs, there appeared to be no point in giving the idea any further consideration. It would be a waste of energy. Jo leaned out and grabbed her bottle of shampoo. She had to focus on anything that didn't involve Tom Caldwell. Washing her hair would do the trick. Her thick brown locks had gotten so long that they were a bit of a chore to wash. Surely something as mundane as hair washing wouldn't trip any memory triggers.

Jo squirted a generous portion of shampoo onto

her hair, then drew her lips down in a disgusted scowl. She had forgotten her body gel. Well, she could use the shampoo for soap, Jo decided. She squeezed a golden bead across her chest and down her abdomen before setting the bottle aside. She tunneled her fingers into her hair and worked the shampoo in. She halted abruptly. Something wasn't right.

Jo pulled her right hand from her hair and stared at the shampoo clinging to her fingers. She scissored her fingers opened and then closed. They stuck together as if her hand was covered in glue. She brought her hand to her nose and sniffed. This wasn't her shampoo. Jo rubbed the thick goo between her fingers.

Realization dawned.

She picked up the shampoo bottle and inspected it more closely, cursing under her breath.

Honey.

Someone had poured out her shampoo and filled the bottle with honey. And now Jo had the stuff squirted in her hair. She glared down at her chest. Not to mention the sticky syrup, now mixed with hot water droplets, oozing down her midsection.

Well, she fumed, there wouldn't be a damned thing sweet about her retaliation.

Maybe charming southern ladies got more flies with honey than they did with vinegar, but hard-ass drill sergeants got what they wanted by marching, crawling, or climbing until they found it.

FIVE

"Sandra Suddath is mine," Jo stated hotly. She shifted in front of Tom's desk to face him more fully.

"Back off, sister," Hattie hissed, "she's mine."

"You're both wrong," Reg snapped, hands on hips, shoulders thrown back for emphasis, "the woman is mine."

"Now hold on just one minute here." Tom looked from one indignant face to the other. This morning's staff meeting had turned into a strategy session on vengeance. "I know Sandra has gotten to all three of you, but the woman belongs to the general, in case you've forgotten."

Reg lifted one unrepentant eyebrow in response and Hattie merely glared at Tom, but Jo looked truly deflated.

"You're right," she said reluctantly. "I would hate to get busted to private and shipped off to the end of nowhere just because I lost my cool with the post commander's wife." Anger flared in those expressive brown eyes. "But it took me almost an hour to wash the honey out of my hair."

That statement resurrected in Tom's mind the erotic fantasy he had struggled to forget all night long. Jo, naked in the shower. The hot spray of water slipping over her smooth skin. The feel of her satiny lips beneath his. The taste of her warm, inviting mouth. Tom forced his focus back to the disgruntled group before him.

"How would you like to be bound and gagged by that heifer?" Hattie growled unrepentantly. She squinted suspiciously at Jo. "I don't get mad, Sergeant Jo, I get even."

"Sounds like a plan to me," Reg added. He folded his arms over his chest as if the issue were settled. "I say we all get even."

"No one"—Tom leaned forward and braced his hands on his desk, shifting his firm gaze from one to the other—"is going to get even. Is that understood?"

Reg rolled his eyes. "Fine."

Hattie snorted.

"Hattie," Tom insisted.

"All right, all right," she groused.

Jo suddenly smiled. "There is *something* we can do," she suggested mysteriously.

All eyes moved to her. Hattie and Reg gazed at Jo with renewed interest; Tom simply looked at her. The memory of last night's kiss played through his head again. How could he want to make love so very badly to a woman who spent the biggest part of her time calling cadence and earning marksmanship awards? But he did. Tom swallowed. He definitely did.

"When a new recruit gets out of line, we intensify his training." Jo nodded thoughtfully, the idea obviously gaining momentum in her pretty little head. "We cut rations and we make them as uncomfortable as possible."

Tom scratched his side as he considered Jo's theory. He'd swabbed the small spot with calamine lotion this morning after showering. Yesterday's time out in the bushes had apparently given him an upclose encounter with something he'd forgotten about. After all the years of training and working at this camp, he had to do something stupid like exposing himself to poison oak. Tom frowned when he realized just how much of a distraction Jo was to him.

"I like the cutting rations part," Hattie enthused with a wicked gleam in her eyes.

"We're doing hair today," Reg said thoughtfully. He cupped his chin in one hand and pursed his lips for a moment, then smiled. "I'm sure I can work a little lesson into my creations. It's amazing what one can do with hairspray and styling gel."

"I've got just the bottle of shampoo you can start with," Jo offered sweetly. She shook her head. "I'll never dump anything onto my hair again without inspecting it first."

Reg settled his hat into place. "Oh, I won't be needing your shampoo, Sergeant Jo." He winked at her. "I have something much more inventive in mind."

"Reg," Tom said carefully. "Don't do anything I'll regret."

Reg looked Tom up and down, then settled a doubtful gaze on him. "You're such a goody-two-shoes. Bet you've never done anything you've regretted." With that, Reg pivoted and marched out the door, leaving Tom to wonder what the hell he meant by that little remark.

"Well." Hattie adjusted her apron, then patted her hairnet. "I imagine I should get breakfast started. Our ladies will be up and around soon." She smiled sheepishly at Jo. "Nothing like a good, hot bowl of plain, unsweetened oatmeal to start your day off right."

Jo returned her smile. "That's the spirit."

Tom waited until Hattie ambled out the door before he turned back to Jo. "Listen, Jo," he began, hoping he could do this without sounding as awkward as he felt at the moment. "I'm really sorry about last night. I was way out of line."

Jo looked away. "We were both out of line." She fixed a hesitant gaze on his. "It won't happen again, Tom. That's the way it has to be."

"You're right," he conceded. "It won't happen again." His gaze lingered on hers, foolishly searching for any sign of hope. "Unless you want it to," he added before he could stop himself.

Those big brown eyes looked away for a second or two, and when her gaze connected with his once more all signs of uncertainty were gone. "I won't," she said firmly.

Disappointment washed over Tom. "All right. I guess I misread your response."

"I guess you did," she retorted coolly. She glanced at the clock on his wall. "I have a formation to get to." She turned and headed for the door.

Tom blew out a disgusted breath and dropped into his chair. Why the hell had he done that? Last night had been a mistake. He knew it. She knew it. Why did he have to try and create an opportunity for another one of those mind-boggling kisses?

Because he was an idiot. An idiot who had suddenly and unexpectedly discovered that, after all this time, he still had real needs. And wants.

But why did the woman he wanted have to be one he couldn't have?

"Tell me one more time why we're doing this, Sergeant Jo," Crystal called out.

Jo glanced over her shoulder but waited until Crystal had low-crawled between two bushes before she answered. "You've mastered most of the exercises designed for weight loss. I thought something new and more physically aggressive might speed up the process," she lied. This was payback . . . pure and simple.

"Oh." Crystal smiled, batting a leafy branch from her face. "I see."

Jo chewed the inside of her cheek to prevent the grin that wanted out every time she looked at the weary group following her. She had gotten them through a pretty tough session that morning. They had done their calisthenics, marched, climbed several small hills, and now the grand finale—low-crawling. But it was Reg who should receive today's gold star. He had given them all hairdos they wouldn't soon forget. Crystal's greatly resembled something Jo had seen on an early Madonna video. Sandra's was a style straight off the Bride of Frankenstein. The rest ranged from Fright Nightish to punk rockish. Leaves, branches and mud from last night's rain stuck to all of them, including Jo.

Sandra and Beulah had spent the morning workout scratching like dogs with fleas, and Jo now had a pretty good idea who had stolen Tom's clothes. The thought that some other woman, even Sandra or Beulah, had seen Tom's glorious body sent a stab of jealousy deep into Jo's chest. She set her jaw and forced the reaction away. She wasn't jealous of Tom.

He wasn't hers.

She swallowed.

And he never would be.

A bloodcurdling scream shattered Jo's worrisome thoughts. She shot to her feet and scanned the women scattered on the ground behind her. Another scream jerked Jo's gaze to the right. Veronica, who had been bringing up the rear all afternoon, had decided to take what she obviously considered a shortcut to catch up. Jo sprinted toward her. They were supposed to follow Jo. That way she cleared the trail a bit for them.

"What's the problem?" she demanded as she surveyed Veronica for any sign of injury.

Veronica hadn't moved. Her eyes were wide with

fright and glued to the ground next to her left hand. Jo saw it then. A snake, partially hidden by the decaying ground cover. She couldn't readily identify it, but Jo knew from the shape of its head that it was poisonous. Jo swore silently.

"Don't move, Veronica." Jo swallowed. "Don't even breathe."

Very slowly, very carefully, Jo eased around to the other side of the snake. With Veronica so close, Jo's only option was to distract the damned thing. She crouched down and rustled the bushes. The snake didn't move. Jo moved closer. Her heart pounded in response to a surge of adrenaline. Snakes were not among her favorite creatures. She eased a tad closer. The snake still didn't react. Jo frowned. The thing should have reacted to her proximity. She looked around for a handy stick but there was nothing. Finally, when she felt confident enough, Jo grabbed the snake and pitched it away from Veronica.

Fortunately, it was already dead.

"Oh God, somebody call 911!" Mildred screamed.

Her heart in her throat, Jo scrambled over to Veronica whom Mildred was now hovering above.

"Oh God, she's had a heart attack!" Mildred ranted.

Jo pushed Mildred aside and then rolled Veronica over. Veronica's eyes fluttered open and she groaned. Jo slumped with relief.

"Everything's fine, Mildred," Jo assured her. "Veronica just fainted, that's all."

"Oh, Sergeant Jo," Veronica cried as she scrambled to a sitting position. "You saved my life." She flung her beefy arms around Jo and hugged her to her bosom.

"It's okay, Veronica." Jo eased out of the woman's hold and drew in a relieved breath.

The women crowded around them. They fussed over Veronica as if she had barely escaped certain death.

"You're a hero, Sergeant Jo," Crystal announced. They all started to talk at once then, agreeing and then praising their savior.

"Don't worry, ladies," Jo assured them when she could get a word in edgewise. "Veronica was never actually in any danger. The snake was dead."

"But, Sergeant Jo," Veronica argued. "You didn't know that until you grabbed that evil serpent by the throat and hurled him over your shoulder. I've never known anyone so brave."

Before Jo could argue, another scream cut through the air. "Help me!" Sandra Suddath squealed.

Jo climbed from the throng of ladies and rushed to where Sandra was still sprawled on the ground between two bushes. "What's wrong, Sandra?"

"It's my hair," she whined. "It's caught in the bushes and I can't get it loose."

Jo surveyed the situation. The big funnel of blond hair atop Sandra's head was tangled in the branches. Jo knelt beside her and reached into the mass of tangles. Her eyes widened in surprise when she touched Sandra's hair. It was as stiff as a poker.

What the hell had Reg used on the woman's hair, spray shellac? Liquid mortar?

"Oh, Sergeant Jo, you've got to get me loose," Sandra bawled as she scratched her back. "I'm itching and muddy and miserable. And I have to pee. Please, Jo, you've just got to get me out of this awful mess."

Jo grinned to herself. She wanted to announce, *now we're even,* but instead, she simply said, "Don't worry, I'll get you out if it's the last thing I do."

Thirty minutes later, Jo had about decided that getting Sandra untangled would be the last thing she ever did. Jo'd had to break some of the smaller branches and leave the loose ends in Sandra's hair. The poor woman looked as if she had wrestled with Mother Nature and lost. Leaves and mud were stuck to her sweatpants and shirt. Tiny branches and their attached leaves stuck out here and there from the cone of super-stiff hair. By the time they made it back to camp, it was dinnertime already.

Sandra had taken one look at the dinner tray Hattie passed to her and its fiber-rich but meager contents, and excused herself early. Veronica had done the same. Jo couldn't say that she blamed the women. They'd had a truly rotten day. Jo smiled. But it was difficult to work up any sympathy for the two.

"You don't think you guys overdid it just a little today, do you, Jo?" Tom scanned the bedraggled group once more, then settled his gaze back on her.

"I'll go a little easier on them tomorrow," Jo relented. She tamped down the feeling that this would all come back to haunt her in the form of a reprimand from the general himself. Jo sighed. This mission would not be a success if the ladies didn't buckle down. One way or another, she had to make the point that discipline was the key to weight loss and good physical conditioning.

Jo glanced down at her empty tray. Hattie's chef salad had been sorely lacking in embellishments, but it was definitely healthy. Jo couldn't recall ever having eaten that much roughage in one sitting before. She grinned again. If she didn't work the weight off the ladies, Hattie would work it *out* of them.

Tom reached across the table, but hesitated just short of touching her. "You have . . ." His fingers brushed at something on her cheek then. Tendrils of heat slid through her at the contact. ". . . mud on your cheek." He smiled, and Jo's heart squeezed.

"Thank you," she said, then looked away from his hopeful gaze. How could she deal with this? Why didn't he just stop looking at her that way? As if he wanted her more than he wanted to take his next breath.

"What's on the agenda for tomorrow?" He leaned back in his chair and folded his arms over his chest. "Mountain climbing?"

Jo stilled. She could feel his long legs on either side of hers. If she shifted even slightly either way, they would touch. She shivered at the thought of feeling his muscled thighs on either side of hers, his full body weight on hers. She could even imagine the sensation of his firm lips, ready for a kiss. Electricity sizzled along her nerve endings at the thought of his wicked tongue invading her mouth. Her feminine muscles tightened when her wild imagination played out what would happen next. Jo jerked herself from the forbidden fantasy and focused on the question he had asked.

"I'm not sure yet," she admitted woodenly. "I don't know what Reg has on his schedule for tomorrow."

Reg was conspicuously absent this evening. Jo wondered if that was a bad sign. Maybe he was afraid to show his face after the outrageous hairdos he had given the ladies. Maybe lynching hadn't gone out of style in Alabama. She touched her throat and swallowed.

"You know there's a new movie playing at the theater tomorrow night. I hear it's gotten great reviews." Tom paused for a significant second. "Maybe we could take a little time off and go see it. That is," he amended with a little shrug, "if you'd like to." He tried hard to act as if her answer didn't matter much one way or another.

Jo smiled sadly. His persistence, not to mention his sincerity, touched her deeply. Too deeply. Why didn't he just forget about her? That way maybe she could forget about him. She looked away and cleared her throat. "That's not a good idea, Tom."

His powerful thighs closed in on Jo's knees. Desire shuddered through her like an earthquake. She turned back to him. He nailed her with a look that told her just how determined he was.

"I knew I didn't misread you," he told her knowingly. "I saw the little hitch in your breathing just then."

"Tom—"

"And you're wrong," he continued. "It is a good idea." He studied her with those amazing blue eyes. "In fact, it's a great idea."

A scream that rattled Jo's teeth halted the argument she was prepared to launch. Dead silence settled over the dining room. Nobody moved.

"The kitchen," Tom suggested, already pushing back from the table.

"Right," Jo muttered as she shot to her feet and raced after Tom who was halfway across the dining room now.

Jo skidded to a halt in the rear of the big kitchen. Tom was kneeling next to a seriously shaken Hattie who lay flat on her back on the tiled floor.

"What happened, Hattie?" Tom asked as he visually inspected her for injury.

Jo knelt on the other side of the pale-as-a-ghost cook. "Are you all right?" Jo pressed.

Hattie looked from Jo to Tom as if she were confused. She lifted her head slightly, then screamed at the top of her lungs again.

"What is it, Hattie?" Tom demanded, concern etched across his handsome face.

Hattie pointed to a shelf beneath a long stainless-steel worktable. Jo and Tom followed her gesture. Both jumped at what they saw. A snake peeked from between two large bowls. Tom swore. Hattie half-scooted, half-crawled away until the wall stopped her.

"Get that thing out of my kitchen," she screeched.

"How the hell did it get in here?" Tom cautiously eased a little closer to the table.

Jo squinted to get a better look. She shook her head slowly from side to side when recognition dawned. "It's okay," she told Tom. Jo leaned forward and pushed aside one of the bowls.

"Wait." Tom jerked her back. Jo lost her balance and fell right in his lap. He held on to her when she would have scrambled away. "It's poisonous," he warned curtly, as if she were dense.

"Don't worry," Jo told him in spite of the sudden tightness of her throat. The feel of his strong thighs beneath her made her heart skip a beat. She moistened her lips and forced her gaze back to the snake. "We've met before. It's dead." Jo hurried from Tom's arms before she changed her mind and snuggled into that inviting embrace. She leaned down and pulled the dead snake from its hiding place and dropped it onto the floor.

Tom, who was standing right beside her now, kicked the snake with the toe of his running shoe. He released a big breath. "It's dead all right."

"And I'll bet I can tell you just who did this, too," Jo said disgustedly. "We ran into this critter this afternoon," she explained.

"You think somebody went back and got him to

scare Hattie?" Tom asked warily. "One of the ladies?"

"That's exactly what I think."

Hattie sidled between Jo and Tom. She bent down
and peered at the dead reptile. She straightened,
hands on hips. She looked from Tom to Jo, outrage
in her gaze. "You do know," she began, "that this
means war!"

SIX

Tom paced the length of his cabin once more. He paused at the front window and stared out at the dark July night. Frustration welled in his chest until he finally shook his head and turned back to the woman standing quietly in the middle of his room. She wasn't helping his frustration level. But there was nothing he could do about that. The next move had to be hers. And Jo still stood staunchly by her all-work-and-no-play motto. Tom blew out another exasperated breath. Right now he had other problems than his sex life, or lack thereof, to resolve.

"I still can't believe they trudged back into those woods and dragged that dead snake back to the kitchen." He raked his fingers through his hair and leaned against the window frame.

Jo folded her arms over her middle and shrugged. "You were the one who thought they were too old for that kind of stuff," she reminded.

"Yeah, yeah, I know." Tom pushed away from the window and walked in Jo's direction. "It won't be the first time I was wrong," he said pointedly, then dropped into his favorite chair. He had been mistaken about Jo, it seemed. He thought she wanted last night's kiss just as much as he did. Could he really have been that wrong?

Tom stared up at Jo, who remained standing. "You could sit down," he offered a little curtly. "It's not like I'm going to attack you or anything."

Huffing a breath of her own frustration, Jo made herself comfortable on the couch directly across the coffee table from him. Tom hadn't seen Jo in anything other than her uniform and the camp's sweatpants and T-shirts. And she looked damned fine in those. But Jo Passerella molded into a faded pair of ragged Levis was breathtaking. The olive drab T-shirt she wore had seen better days as well, but it molded Jo's small, firm breasts like a second skin. He was pretty damned sure she wasn't wearing a bra. That alone made this meeting as frustrating as hell. Why couldn't he simply have a conversation with the woman without noticing . . .

Tom swallowed hard. Her hair was down, too. Really down—no braid, no bun. It draped her shoulders just as he had imagined it would. The long, silky stuff still looked damp here and there. Tom had been furious when he had stormed over to her cabin and demanded an immediate meeting. Jo informed him that she had just returned from the shower and that she would come to his cabin as soon as humanly possible.

Five minutes later, she knocked on his door. Tom felt like a complete heel now for allowing his anger to get the better of him. He wasn't mad at Jo. Hell, he wasn't mad at anybody really. All he could think about at the moment, with those big brown eyes staring at him, was how he would like to make love to this little sergeant. Right now. Right here.

"You said you wanted to talk," she reminded when he continued to stare at her without speaking.

"Look." Tom leaned forward and propped his elbows on his spread knees. "I know the ladies have apologized profusely to Hattie. And I know they didn't mean any real harm, but what if Hattie had hurt herself when she fell?" He frowned, thinking about what might've happened. "Or worse, she could have had a heart attack. Hattie isn't a young woman."

Jo shrugged. "I don't know what else to do. No one will admit who actually did it. They're taking the blame as a group. I do have my suspicions." Jo thought for a minute. "I can't, in good conscience, work them any harder than I already am. If we complain to the general, it'll look as if we can't handle the job."

Tom spotted something in Jo's eyes that made his gut clench. She was seriously worried. "Wait a minute, Jo," he said cautiously. "You don't think I'd complain to the general without talking to you first, do you?"

"I guess I couldn't blame you if you did. The ladies have been truly obnoxious. And I feel responsible." She averted her gaze so he wouldn't read the rest of what was likely running through her mind.

If anything went wrong, Jo would take the heat. She would be held responsible, Tom realized with profound clarity. No way would he let that happen. He stood, took the three steps that separated them, and sat down on the edge of the coffee table. He rested his elbows on his knees once more and settled his gaze firmly onto hers, whether she liked it or not.

"Jo, we're in this together. I hope you understand that," he said quietly. "I asked to have a drill sergeant assigned here and I'm not going to let you take the blame for anything alone."

Jo stared at her hands. She nervously twisted and untwisted her fingers. "Thank you, but those women are my responsibility. I—"

Tom covered her fidgeting hands with his. She watched as his fingers closed around hers. Her hands felt so small and delicate within his big, rough ones. A protective feeling that overwhelmed all else bloomed in his heart. "I'm the director of this camp. They're my responsibility, too. And Reg's and Hattie's," he reminded her.

Jo finally met his gaze again. She looked at him for a long time before she spoke. Tom saw the uncertainty, the worry that she tried to hide. But it was the desire that made his heart stumble. He hadn't been wrong about her response to his kiss. Tom had the sudden urge to do a little end-zone victory dance, but he held himself in check. Jo had more to say. And he was far from getting her to admit her feelings to herself.

"Tom, I appreciate what you're saying." She swallowed, the effort visible along the column of her lovely throat. "But that's not the way the Army does things. I cannot fail in this mission." She pressed him with her gaze, trying to make him understand. "It's just not an option. I've probably already offended the general's wife."

Tom wanted to reassure her, he really did. But he couldn't speak. He couldn't even breathe. There was something about the way her hair fell across her cheek when she tilted her head, the way her eyes turned an ever darker shade of brown when she looked deeply into his eyes. And the way her fingers clasped his . . . there was just something about Jo that made Tom ache for some . . . *thing* he couldn't name.

"We won't fail," he managed past the lump in his throat. "I promise."

She smiled. And Tom's heart rejoiced. The smile was completely unguarded and totally beautiful.

"You can't promise that," she argued, her voice trembling with the emotion now shining in her eyes. She wasn't smiling anymore. Her expression was as fiercely intent as his must be.

"I just did," he murmured. Tom's gaze moved down to her lips, which were full, lush, and tempting beyond what any man could bear. But he couldn't kiss her.

"Tom." One small hand pulled free of his and came up to touch his jaw.

Tom closed his eyes and savored the feel of her fingers on his skin.

"Why do you do this to me?" she murmured.

The ache he heard in her voice mirrored his own. He opened his eyes and connected with the desperation in those dark mesmerizing depths. "I just can't help myself, Jo. Try to understand . . ."

Tom knew the moment Jo surrendered. The need, the desire, the tenderness—it was all right there in her eyes. Somehow her lips found his. The kiss was slow, easy, and sweet. But when her fingers threaded into his hair, Tom had to have more . . . had to be closer. He dropped to his knees on the floor and pushed between her thighs.

Jo took full control of the kiss then. Pulling him closer, thrusting her soft tongue inside his mouth. Tom touched her hair first, stroking the silky stuff down over her firm breasts. His groin tightened unmercifully when his fingertips touched her nipples. Jo moaned into his mouth and the sound twisted his insides, made him crazy with savage need. He flattened his palms against her slender ribcage and concentrated on the feel of her sweet lips against his.

She leaned back, pulling Tom with her, kissing him passionately. The heat at the apex of her thighs burned into him. He wanted to touch her there, but it was too soon. His hands slipped down to the bottom of her T-shirt and pushed the fabric upward. She arched toward him, urging him on. He pressed his erection against her, grinding their bodies together. The feel of her satiny skin undid him completely.

Tom pulled free of the kiss and lowered his mouth. Jo encouraged him by pressing him more firmly against her. He rained kisses over her breasts, enjoying the womanly taste of her. He teased her nipples, tugging gently until Jo cried in pleasurable agony, then he took one into his mouth and sucked long and hard.

"Tom . . . oh, God, Tom."

Tom drew back far enough to pull the shirt over her head. He watched as her long, dark hair tumbled over her shoulders, then over her swollen breasts. Jo reached for his shirt next, tugging it up and off. She tossed it to the floor with her own. Her soft fingers caressed his chest, touching, learning.

He closed his eyes and stifled the groan that rose in his throat. When her hot mouth closed over his left nipple, he roared with need. His hands fisted in her hair, urging her closer, telegraphing his need for more. He reached for her breasts, squeezed them, stimulating the pebbled peaks with his thumbs. She teased him with her teeth, her tongue, then sucked until sweat broke out across his forehead. Tom wasn't sure how much more he could take. She was driving him mad. It had been too long since he had allowed himself this kind of pleasure . . . he wanted Jo too much.

He closed his fingers around her tiny waist and urged Jo to her feet. She moaned a slight protest, but obeyed. As she watched him, he unbuttoned her jeans, then lowered the zipper. Her breath caught when he slipped his hands inside and pushed the soft denim and satin panties from her hips. Tom took a long moment to admire the beauty of Jo's utterly feminine body. She shivered when his ragged breath fanned across her sensitive mound. He restrained the need to take her now . . . this had to be special. He had to move slowly. Very, very slowly.

Lifting first one foot and then the other, Tom removed Jo's shoes. With the shoes gone, he removed her jeans and panties in the same manner. Then he sat back on his heels and took in all of her. Desire swelled his manhood, urging him to take her.

Jo was beautiful. Her eyes were closed, her lips parted slightly. Her breasts rose and fell with her rapid intake of breath. Unable to hold back a moment longer, Tom pressed a kiss between her breasts. Slowly, taking great pains, he kissed each rib on his journey downward. His tongue dipped inside her navel, then lower, and lower. He nuzzled her intimately until she groaned with pleasure.

Tom wrapped his arms around Jo then and lowered her to the floor. Her heart felt as if it might burst from her chest at any moment. He brushed a fleeting kiss across her lips, then left her. Jo opened her eyes to see where he had gone. In one fluid motion he removed his sweatpants and briefs. She watched the smooth flex and contraction of his muscles as he moved. His body was every bit as perfect as she remembered. Jo held her breath as he knelt between her thighs. Between that golden hair, those piercing blue eyes, and all that muscle, he looked like a Greek god intent on his latest erotic conquest.

His gaze lingered on hers for the briefest moment, his expression fierce. He leaned forward then, braced his hands on either side of her waist and dipped his head down to take her breast again. Jo clutched at the soft rug beneath her. He suckled until desire coiled so tightly within her that she cried out with the exquisite pain of sexual longing. Tom gave equal attention to her other breast, heightening her erotic tension. And then he moved lower. He spread her legs further apart and pressed his mouth to the part of her that throbbed with the need he had elicited. There he teased—and pleased—until she felt ready to shatter like the most fragile glass.

He moved over her then, his lips on her shoulder, her throat, then sealing completely over hers. Jo pushed her arms around his lean waist and pulled his closer. His tongue thrust into her mouth. Her legs entwined with his. His hand moved between them, and his fingers stroked flesh so sensitive that Jo lost her breath completely. He guided himself to the delicate folds of her feminine core, and the first nudge of his erection sent fire rushing through her veins. He thrust within her ever so slowly, the nearly unbearable sensation wrenching a savage cry from both of them. Then he held absolutely still for two long beats. Jo climaxed on his next thrust. The waves of pure pleasure rocked her to her very soul.

But that wasn't enough for Tom. He lifted her bottom, pushing more deeply inside her. The building tension started anew. Each powerful thrust, each kiss of his lips pushed her closer and closer to another peak. Jo squeezed her eyes shut and tried to hold back—to wait for him. But she couldn't. Her body responded to him on a level that was beyond all control. Climax crashed down around her once more, and this time the rhythmic throbbing and clenching went on and on until Tom's body jerked with the first throes of release. He drove into her once, twice more, and then his body arched like a bow and his own powerful climax claimed him.

Tom rolled to her side, pulling Jo against him. For a long time they could only struggle for breath. There was no strength to speak. Jo closed her eyes and replayed every perfect moment. She had only made love twice before and neither occasion had come close to this. Tom was a skilled lover, that was clear. A twinge of inadequacy skittered through her. Could she have possibly pleased him half as much as he pleased her?

"Jo," he murmured against her hair, then pressed a tender kiss there. "You are so beautiful . . . so perfect. No one has ever made me feel this way before."

A delicious glow replaced all her doubts. She had

pleased Tom. At the moment that was the most important thing in the world to her.

But what about tomorrow?

After PT the next morning, Jo dismissed the decidedly reserved ladies. No one whined or complained about anything, not even the three-mile walk, which was accomplished in record time. Jo wasn't sure whether she should be relieved or suspicious. Whatever the case, the ladies would be Reg's problem for the next two hours.

Jo tried to force away the thoughts of last night's lovemaking, but she couldn't. Little thrills of desire zinged her each time she thought of Tom's incredible loving. Or of his amazing body. Her cheeks turned pink each time she considered just how intimate his lovemaking had been. No man had ever touched her in that way. Her pulse reacted every time she thought of him. He had begged her to stay the night with him, but she couldn't allow herself that much freedom. Getting emotionally involved was all too great a risk. Jo didn't want to know what it felt like to awaken next to Tom bright and early in the morning. She didn't want to risk his wanting to make love again. Their one encounter would haunt her for the rest of her life. The moment he had fallen asleep, she had left him.

It was the right thing to do.

No matter how much it hurt to do it, or even to think about it now, she had been right to leave. Jo couldn't count on anything that had happened last night. Discipline was the key. She would keep this relationship on a strictly professional basis from now on, one way or another. She had to . . . it was her only hope of protecting her heart.

"Jo!" a male voice whispered.

Jo looked around. A hand extending from the bushes only a few feet away motioned for her to come. Frowning, Jo walked slowly in that direction.

"Reg?" she asked hesitantly as she inspected the perfectly manicured hand more closely.

When she paused near the cluster of greenery, the hand grabbed her by the arm and pulled her inside. Jo swallowed the scream that rose in her throat.

"You have to help me, Jo, I have a *big* problem."

Jo squeezed her eyes shut. She absolutely would not look. If someone had stolen Reg's clothes—Jo shuddered—she didn't want to know. She positively did not want to see Reg naked. No way.

"I don't know what I'm going to do," he fretted. "This is a disaster. I should have seen it coming after all that's happened."

He was silent for a moment. Jo didn't even breathe. She stood stock still and kept her eyes shut so tight her face hurt.

"Jo," Reg continued, his tone oddly high-pitched. "Why are your eyes closed?"

Jo chewed her lower lip for a sec, trying to think how to answer his question. "No offense, Reg, but if someone has stolen your clothes, just say so and I'll go get you some more." She wished he would hurry. The effort of keeping her eyes closed so tightly was growing more and more difficult by the second.

Reg made an impatient sound in his throat. "No one has stolen my clothes," he said indignantly. "I haven't taken them off."

Jo opened her eyes, then blinked rapidly. Reg's face, flushed with irritation, came into focus. Jo breathed a sigh of relief when her gaze verified that he was, in fact, fully dressed. "Sorry, Reg, I thought—"

"Never mind that," he snapped. "You have to help me." Desperation swiftly replaced his irritation.

"What's the problem?" Worry drew Jo's brows together. What had they done now? Whatever it was, it had Reg in a real panic.

"I found this note on my door this morning." He quickly unfolded the wrinkled paper in his hand. "At first I didn't think too much of it, but as I was showering I started to think about the snake and"— Reg shuddered visibly—"I decided I couldn't risk it."

Jo reread the boldly scrawled words on the page. *Watch your back*, the note warned.

"You think one of the ladies sent you this note?"

Reg rolled his eyes and flung his arms heavenward. "Well, who else would have? I'm certain Hattie didn't. You didn't send it, did you?"

"Of course not." Jo scowled. This was definitely going too far.

"It had to be one of them. How can I conduct

my class and watch my back too?" he demanded, his hysteria rising. "That's impossible."

Jo shrugged. "No problem. I'll sit in on your class today. Is that what you want me to do?"

Reg's relief was palpable. "Yes, thank you."

"No big deal." Jo smiled. "Let's go make those ladies beautiful."

"I'm not a miracle worker," he muttered. Reg held back a bush so Jo could exit, then he followed. He insisted that Jo go into the classroom first and see that it was safe for him to come inside. Still a little uncertain herself, she stepped through the door. An immediate hush fell over the ladies when they spotted Jo.

"Good morning again, ladies."

"Good morning, Sergeant Jo," they chimed, all smiling pleasantly. Too pleasantly.

Jo leaned back through the still open door. "It's okay, come on in," she whispered to Reg. She took a seat near the door where she could keep an eye out for trouble, or make a hasty run for help if necessary.

After clearing his throat rather loudly, Reg strutted into the room. Jo watched the ladies, making sure nobody made any sudden moves. The whole lot of them sat perfectly still and as quiet as church mice. Jo caught a glimpse of Reg in her peripheral vision as he skirted his desk. She did a double take, then frowned. Before she could decide if she had seen what she thought she saw, Reg turned and quickly wrote several notes on the board for the class's information. Enthusiastic giggles teetered through his attentive students.

Jo's eyes widened in disbelief, but she had to bite her lower lip hard to prevent her own chuckle. Written across Reg's back in big, bold red letters were the words *Somebody Kiss Me!*

"Oh, teacher!" Sandra Suddath called cheerily.

Jo eyed Sandra suspiciously. What was she up to? Maybe Jo should interrupt Reg right now and warn him. She opened her mouth to speak but he cut her off.

"Yes, Sandra?" he drawled impatiently.

"Why are you writing those words up there?" Sandra gestured toward the front of the room.

Reg looked heavenward and made a tsking sound. "I'm writing you a list of things to do in order to learn the proper application of concealer and foundation. Taking notes would be advisable."

"So we're supposed to follow your instructions?" Sandra prompted.

"To the letter," he said tartly. "Whatever written instruction I put before you in this classroom, you are to do without question."

Before Jo could get his attention, a dozen ladies had clamored around Reg and were following the instructions written on his back.

To the letter.

"So they all kissed you, huh?" Tom asked with a wide grin. He took a forkful of salad and chewed to cover his amusement. He would have given a month's salary to have seen it, but just hearing Jo's description was funny enough.

Reg looked up from his lunch tray and shot Tom a withering glare. "It wasn't the slightest bit amusing," he snapped. "I'm certain I need a tetanus booster." He stabbed a cherry tomato. "Or perhaps a rabies shot."

Tom leaned forward and assessed Reg's neck. "Man, I think you missed a spot." He gestured to a tiny smudge of bright pink lipstick near Reg's collar. "What's your wife going to think?"

Color racing up his neck, Reg swiped at the smudge with his napkin. "Subject change," he announced crossly, his tone considerably higher than usual.

Tom turned to Jo, who sat next to Reg on the opposite side of the table. "How was your morning, Jo?" His insides turned immediately to mush when those big brown eyes focused on him. God, he had it bad for the lady. One night of passion and he was in love.

Tom swallowed.

Had he just said *love*?

He shook himself.

"Fine." She offered a hint of smile. "And yours?" she returned politely.

So that was the way it would be. Tom sighed inwardly. "Fine," he replied with forced nonchalance. "Just fine." He didn't know whether to be relieved or scared to death. He couldn't decide how he should feel. One moment he thought he was okay, then the next—

Jo glanced at him, then quickly looked the other way.

Tom would have given anything to know what she was thinking. It bugged the hell out of him that she had gotten up and left his bed in the middle of the night. He supposed it was for the best, but somehow that didn't make it right with him. He wasn't sure anything would ever be right with him again.

"Surprise, ladies!"

All eyes moved to the front of the dining room. Hattie was grinning like a Cheshire cat and displaying a huge, luscious-looking chocolate cake. Tom's mouth dropped open. Hattie had wanted to scalp the whole lot of them. What was this all about?

"As a peace offering, I've made you ladies this big, rich chocolate cake." Oohs and awes punctuated the cook's announcement. "I say we make amends." Hattie produced an even wider smile.

Tom had a bad feeling about this. A very bad feeling. What on earth was Hattie up to?

Tom, Reg, and Jo watched, stupefied, as Hattie served each lady a big slab of the decadent-looking cake. His stomach rumpled in anticipation.

"Ummmm," Jo hummed. "Chocolate's my favorite. I think I'll have a slice."

"None for me." Reg patted his flat stomach. "I have to watch my weight."

Jo looked to Tom. He shrugged as if he didn't care one way or another. "Why not?" Cake or no, at least he would get to walk across the room with Jo. He would eat dirt for that pleasure.

Jo and Tom waited while Hattie served the last of the ladies. When she finally turned to them, Tom said, "Hattie, that was awfully thoughtful of you."

Jo grabbed a saucer and extended it toward the cook. "I'll take a nice big slice, please."

"Sorry, I just served the last piece."

Jo frowned. "Oh, come on, Hattie, you have to have another slice in that kitchen somewhere."

Hattie leaned forward and gave Jo and Tom a sly look. "Trust me, you ain't missing a thing."

SEVEN

Later that afternoon Jo stood before her one remaining retreat participant and watched in amazement as the other eleven made yet another mad dash to the latrine. Sandra and Mildred were pushing in front of the others as if their lives depended upon getting through the door first. Jo frowned, wondering if they were slacking again, or if they were really sick. She crossed her arms over her chest and considered another possibility.

The cake.

Hattie had assured Jo that she wasn't missing anything by not eating any of the cake. Maybe there was more to that advice than Jo had first thought.

Jo turned to Crystal. "Did you have any of Hattie's cake?"

Crystal shook her head adamantly. "I'm allergic to chocolate."

A few minutes later, the other women trudged back to the formation. Most were holding their stomachs and looked like the wind had been sucked from their sails.

Jo surveyed the solemn-faced group. "If we're all ready now, ladies, we'll head out on our scheduled three-mile walk."

Sandra's eyes suddenly rounded in horror. She grabbed her stomach and groaned, then ran as fast as she could back to the latrine.

Jo tried to work up a little concern, but it was hard in coming. "Perhaps we'll wait a few more minutes," she offered to the others.

"Sergeant Jo, I think I need to go lie down," Veronica whined. "I'm not feeling so well."

"Me either," Mildred chimed in.

"Oh, Lord!" Beulah broke from formation and sprinted in the direction Sandra had disappeared.

Jo heaved a resigned sigh. "Let's call it an afternoon then," she announced. "The next formation will be at 0600 tomorrow."

Jo watched with only a flicker of sympathy as most of them hurried toward the latrine. Tom wasn't going to like this. And there was no way she could keep it from him. He would want to know why the ladies weren't taking their scheduled hike. She should never have started providing him with daily agendas.

At that precise moment, Jo looked up to find the subject of her worrisome thoughts watching her from the door to his office. Judging by the look on his handsome face, he was anything but happy.

Tom glared first at Jo, then Reg, and finally at Hattie. Jo braced herself for the storm. She had not seen him this angry. A muscle flexed rhythmically in his tense jaw. His hands on his hips, he looked away and then paced the length of his office once more. Jo had the distinct impression that he was trying to get a grip on his anger before he erupted, his fury descending upon them like hot lava.

He pivoted and retraced his steps, pausing before them once more. Tom shook his head slowly from side to side. "I cannot believe you did this, Hattie," he finally said. His voice was deeper, harder than normal. His crystal blue eyes burned with irritation. "You've worked at this camp for twenty years."

"And you." Tom turned to Reg. "Putting the idea in her head. I can't believe a grown man and woman would conspire to do such a thing."

Unflappable, Hattie rocked her chair back on two legs and glared up at Tom. "Served 'em right as far as I'm concerned."

"Here, here," Reg agreed. He folded his arms over his chest and gave Tom an indignant glare. "I agree without reservation."

Tom turned to Jo then, his features taut. "Is that the way you feel, too, Jo?"

Jo looked from Hattie to Reg. Both gave her an evil look, daring her to disagree. "Well," Jo began as she shifted her gaze to Tom, who was technically her boss, "Reg and Hattie do have a point." She shrugged. "After the snake scare—"

"Don't forget the way they mauled me," Reg piped in with a shudder.

"And . . . and the kissing incident, it's true that the ladies did deserve exactly what they got." Jo cleared her throat beneath Tom's intensifying stare. "However—" Reg and Hattie glowered at her. "However," Jo continued, "we are adults and our behavior recently has been . . . well . . . somewhat juvenile, don't you think?" she added weakly.

"Exactly," Tom stated succinctly.

"Traitor," Reg muttered from the corner of his mouth.

"Brownnoser," Hattie mumbled beneath her breath.

Jo shot them both an appalled look.

"You see." Tom waved his arms magnanimously. "You're behaving like children. As bad as the kids who are required to attend this camp."

Reg heaved an exaggerated breath. He waved one hand airily. "Fine. We've behaved badly. What are you going to do, Tom?" He shot Tom a challenging look. "Spank us or send us to the corner?"

Tom cocked that gorgeous head of his and smiled one of those smiles that took the breath right out of Jo's lungs. Every square inch of his incredibly male body cried out to her. Jo's errant gaze roved over more than six feet of pure heaven. She swallowed tightly and forced herself to study the row of trophies behind his desk. She absolutely would not connect spanking with Tom.

"You know, Reg, I've given that quite a bit of thought," Tom said slowly. "Since today is Friday, I've decided to cancel passes for tonight. Nobody leaves the camp. That includes staff."

Reg was outraged. "You can't mean it. That's ridiculous!"

"I ain't missed a Friday night movie in forty years," Hattie growled.

"Well, you're missing one tonight. Tonight there will be no passes for any of you or the ladies. And there'll be no dessert of any kind, no television, no radio, no cards, no nothing." With a look that cut to the bone, Tom dared them to argue.

"Fine," Reg snipped.

Tom turned to Hattie.

Hattie poked out her bottom lip and pouted.

"Hattie?" Tom asked.

"Can I catch the matinee tomorrow afternoon?"

Tom closed his eyes and let out a sigh. "Yes, you can go to the matinee tomorrow afternoon."

"All right, then," the cook agreed, her face lit up and happy.

Jo smiled. Tom was a pushover when it came to the people he cared about. That's one of the things that made him so lovable, Jo realized. She stilled and her smile drooped. She couldn't love Tom. She couldn't love anybody right now. She had to focus on her career.

"Well, if Hattie gets to go to the matinee, I'm getting the afternoon off too," Reg was demanding as he and Hattie left Tom's office.

Jo stood quickly. She had been so lost in her troubling thoughts she hadn't even realized the two were leaving. She should be going as well.

"What about you, Jo?"

Tom's deep voice wrapped around her and made her want to close her eyes and forget all about snakes, cakes, and other camp-related craziness.

Jo lifted her gaze to the man who was looking down at her so very intently. Her heart thumped with anticipation. If he only knew the power he held over her.

"What do you want?"

Oh, that was a loaded question if Jo had ever heard one. What did she want? She wanted Tom Caldwell in her arms. She wanted him to kiss her the way he did last night. She wanted him to make love to her in that slow, thorough manner of his, leaving them both sated. She wanted to spend an entire night in his arms, and to wake up with him every morning for the rest of her life.

Jo froze. Five days she had known this man. And in that five days they had gone from being strangers to being lovers . . . and now he possessed a big chunk of her carefully guarded heart. Fear surged through her. This couldn't be real. She had to be blowing the whole thing way out of proportion.

"Jo, are you all right?"

She met his worried gaze. Dear Lord, she had made a serious mistake. How could she have presumed she wouldn't become attached to him?

"Jo?"

She blinked rapidly. "Im fine." Jo shook her head. "I don't want anything." She had to get out of here. She was confused. She needed to think.

"Jo, wait." Tom pulled her back around to face him. His strong hand held her arm firmly in its grasp as if he feared she might run away. "We need to talk about last night," he said softly.

Tom was right to hold on to her. Had he not, Jo

would have run out of his office as fast as she could. She was totally unprepared.

"What's to talk about?" Jo held his gaze, hard as that proved, hoping like hell he couldn't read the truth in hers. This had to stop now.

Hurt flickered in his eyes at her words, and Jo wished with all her heart she could take them back. But she couldn't. She had to stand firm.

"Look, Tom." Jo steeled herself against the emotions tugging at her. She didn't want to feel any of this. And the only way to keep it from going any further was to stop it. Now. "We shouldn't make too much out of what happened," she continued. Her voice sounded as hollow as she felt. "We crossed the line. It was a mistake. You have your life. I have mine. They're worlds apart and there's no place to meet in the middle."

Tom's grip tightened on her arm. That tic started in his chiseled jaw once more. "That's not a problem. How about we meet right here?" He jerked Jo against him and kissed her long and hard.

Jo's bravado wilted beneath his sensual assault. How would she ever fight him when he used such overpowering weapons? His arms went around her and he deepened the almost punishing kiss. Jo reminded herself to struggle, but the only thing her hands would do was tangle in his thick hair. A desire so fierce filled her that all else ceased to matter. There was only Tom and the way he was kissing her . . . and the way she was kissing him back.

When he at last released her, Jo touched her swollen mouth. Her lips burned with the heat he had generated. No one had ever kissed her like that.

"You were saying," he murmured breathlessly.

Still cradled in his strong arms, Jo braced her hands against his massive chest. She had to get a handle on herself. If one week with Tom was this devastating to her self-control, how would she ever get through the next several weeks and meet the general's expectations?

"We hardly know each other," she argued, wishing he wouldn't look at her that way, as if she was everything he had ever wanted and more.

"I was born in Waynesville and I've lived here all my life. You already know about my family. I've never been married or engaged, mainly because I've always been too busy," he said with a grin. "I teach high school history. I own a house, a jeep, and right now I'm kind of between dogs."

Jo frowned. *Between dogs.*

As if reading her mind, he added, "The dog I'd had for ten years, who came to camp with me every summer for the past five, died last winter." Sadness flickered in his eyes. "I'm having a hard time finding a new one." He shrugged. "Maybe I haven't really been looking."

"You didn't tell me," Jo said, her eyes a little misty. "Nobody mentioned you'd just lost your dog."

Tom shrugged one broad shoulder. "Everyone's been really careful not to mention him."

"What kind of dog was he?"

Tom smiled, obviously remembering. "Jack was a

big brown Lab who did nothing but eat and sleep."
He laughed softly. "But I loved him anyway."

Jo's defenses crumbled like a sand castle on a
stretch of lonely beach. "I'm sorry," she offered sin-
cerely.

Another sad smile tugged at one corner of his
mouth. "I'll get over Jack. It's you that worries me."

"Tom." Jo searched his gaze, looking for anything besides all that intensity. Did he have to be
so serious? Wasn't it enough that her heart would
be broken? Did he have to prove to her that his
would be as well? "You're making this awfully hard
on me," she told him. She wouldn't tell him just
how hard.

He grinned wickedly. "It's pretty damned hard for
me too." One strong hand slid down to her bottom
and pressed Jo intimately against the evidence of
his statement. He was fully aroused.

Before Jo could rally an appropriate response, he
went on, "Just promise me that you won't pretend
last night didn't happen. Promise me," he pressed,
"that you'll keep an open mind about us."

Us?

Jo's entire being reacted to his words. Had last
night meant as much to him as it had to her? Could
it have affected him half as deeply?

"Promise me, Jo," he whispered insistently.

"I promise," Jo heard herself say.

"We'll seal it with a kiss," he murmured against
her lips. His arms tightened around her waist. His
mouth closed firmly over hers.

And Jo stopped thinking at all.

* * *

Tom sat on the steps outside his cabin door and stared at the star-filled sky. He thought about all that he had said to Jo. He wondered if it would make a difference. Tom leaned back against the closed door and asked himself again if he really wanted it to. What was it about Jo that made him think about forever? She was so damned determined to make her way in this world all by herself. To prove that she was as big and tough as anyone else. That was part of what drew Tom to her. And beneath all that attitude was a soft, vulnerable woman who responded to him as if she were his long-lost soul mate.

Jo wouldn't be here nearly long enough for them to really get to know each other. Could he simply let her go when camp was over for the summer? Tom frowned. He didn't think he could.

Tom tried again to get to the bottom of what it was that made Jo different. What made him want her so very much? It wasn't as if he hadn't had girlfriends in the past. He'd had his share. But this time was different. He felt different about Jo . . . somehow. Making love with her had been mind-blowing, but it wasn't enough. He wanted more . . . and then some more after that. He had always assumed that falling in love happened slowly, over an extended period of time with two people who knew each other well. Only teenagers fell in love at first sight.

Disgusted with himself for overanalyzing the situation, Tom pushed to his feet and started his usual nightly routine of walking the grounds. Even if it was considerably later than usual.

Tom slid his hands into his pockets and strolled at a leisurely pace. No point in hurrying. He sure as hell didn't have anything to rush back to. His thoughts went immediately to Jo, and last night. He wondered what it would be like to make love with her again. Could it possibly be that amazing the next time? Tom had a feeling that every time with Jo would be like the first time. And he wanted so badly to test that theory that he ached with the need of it. Ached for her.

He stopped, closed his eyes and allowed the night sounds to envelop him. The gentle breeze rustling the leaves of the trees, the crickets crying for more rain, and Jo's feminine laughter.

Tom's eyes snapped open. He spun around. He surveyed the darkness for any sign of Jo. Then he spotted the light on in her cabin. Tom walked slowly toward that beacon. He couldn't have stopped himself if he had tried. As he neared, he could see Jo sitting in a chair next to the lamp. The window was open and the wind shifted the worn curtains hanging on either side of the sash. A book in her hand, Jo appeared lost in whatever fantasy the author had woven.

Knowing he shouldn't, but doing it anyway, Tom climbed the steps and knocked on her door. He braced his hands on the door frame and waited for her to answer. When the door swung inward, he wasn't fully prepared for the impact of Jo completely relaxed. Her long dark hair hung loose around her shoulders. An oversized T-shirt served as a nightgown, and she was barefoot. This was the Jo he wanted to see every night. The real woman behind the uniform and the take-charge attitude. The one that had haunted his dreams from the moment she'd emerged from that cloud of dust. The same one who had stolen his heart right out of his chest.

"Is something wrong?" Jo asked, concern shadowing her soft eyes.

"No, everything's fine." He knew he was staring but he couldn't stop looking at her.

She licked those perfect lips, then chewed on the lower one. Tom's breath caught in his chest. "I heard you laughing," he finally said. His gaze locked on hers. Those huge brown eyes shone with uncertainty, but even all that hesitancy couldn't hide the flicker of desire he saw there, which mirrored his own.

Jo smiled. Her cheeks flushed. Something near Tom's heart shifted at the sweet gesture. She flashed the cover of the book she was holding. "I was reading. You didn't ban that for the night."

His grin started in one corner, but quickly spread across his lips. Tom reached for her hand and took another look at the book she had been reading. A man and woman entwined in each other's arms beneath a full moon graced the sexy cover.

"Romance?" he asked, surprised. "I would never have figured you for a romance reader. Doesn't exactly fit with the combat boots."

"I borrowed it," she said quickly, as if embarrassed that she had been caught.

Tom supposed that romance novels and military training had little to do with each other. And he was more than sure that getting caught reading one by her male peers was not something she planned to allow. Her explanation suddenly resounded in his head. *Borrowed it?*

Tom pinned her with a curious look. "I didn't know Hattie read romance."

Jo cleared her throat. "Actually, it belongs to Reg."

Tom did a double take. "Reg?"

Jo shrugged noncommittally. "He said something about he and his wife acting—" She made a face. "You don't really want to know."

Tom shook his head. "I think you're right. I don't want to know."

"Is there something you need?"

And she, Tom considered, didn't really want to know the answer to that question either. Because the only thing he needed was her.

He shoved his hands into his pockets. He looked back toward his own dark cabin, then shook his head. "Nothing. I was just out . . . walking." His gaze settled on hers again.

Jo glanced up at the dark sky. "It's a perfect night for walking."

He took that opportunity to admire her beautiful profile. "Perfect," he agreed.

Her gaze collided with his and desire sparked hot and fierce between them.

"Tom—"

"I know," he relented. "I should go." He looked down. Anger swirled deep in his gut at her refusal to allow what they had started to go any further. Tom took a step back before returning his gaze to hers. "We wouldn't want to make another mistake." He turned, took the final step down, and walked away.

"Wait."

Tom stopped. He didn't turn around, though.

Jo came around in front of him, forcing him to look her in the eye. "Don't punish me because I live by a different set of rules than you do. It would never work, Tom. Trust me, I've seen too many couples try and fail. The ones who make it are few and far between. One night of explosive passion isn't going to change that."

His lips twitched. "Explosive?"

Jo looked away and heaved an exasperated sigh. "You are incorrigible, Tom Caldwell, do you know that?"

Tom smiled then. He couldn't let that one go. "Is that what you learned in that book?" He pointed to the paperback still clutched in her hand. "You thought last night was explosive?"

She shook her head, braced her hands on her slim hips and looked up at him. "Yes." Jo pushed past him and stalked back toward her cabin.

"Jo."

She turned around slowly. So slowly that the moonlight shimmered on her hair. The light from her open cabin door silhouetted her petite frame through the thin white cotton of her T-shirt.

Tom's physical reaction shook him hard. "Explosive is a good description," he agreed.

Muffled voices splintered the tension that connected them. Tom turned toward the sound.

"Did you hear voices?"

Jo was right beside him, staring into the darkness just as intently.

"Yeah, I did," he said slowly. Tom squinted to make out any movement in the darkness. Nothing moved.

"Over here, over here!" a seemingly disembodied voice exclaimed in a loud whisper.

Taking care not to make even the slightest sound, Tom and Jo eased forward in the direction of the voice they had heard.

"Wait, wait! I can do it!"

Tom would know that voice anywhere. Sandra Suddath. Jo apparently realized the same, judging by the murderous look on her face.

"What is she up to now?" Jo hissed.

"I wouldn't even try to hazard a guess," Tom muttered under his breath. He stopped outside the cabin that served as his office to listen again. The voices were slightly louder now.

Jo peeked cautiously around the corner, then jerked as if she'd been startled. "Oh . . . my . . . God," she said, her voice dripping with disbelief.

Tom leaned past her. He had to look twice to be sure of what he saw. Sandra Suddath and two of her buddies were crowded around the gate. Sandra was trying desperately to climb to the top of the twelve-foot gate. The metal structure shifted a bit beneath her weight and unskilled climbing tactics.

Tom frowned. "What the hell are they doing? Trying to escape?" Tom made a tight choking sound at the his own gaffe. This wasn't a prison. They didn't have to escape. The ladies were here of their own free will. The only people who needed to escape were his staff.

Jo tugged him closer. "Look right there." She pointed to the narrow gap between Mildred and Beulah. "Do you see it?"

Tom scrubbed a hand over his face. "Well, I'll be damned." He saw it all right. A Domino's Pizza delivery boy waited on the other side of the gate.

"Lady, I ain't climbing no fence, no matter how big the tip is," the kid holding the pizza said flatly. "Are you coming over for it, or what?"

"Just keep your shorts on," Sandra scolded. "I'm coming over."

"Excuse me, ladies, is there a problem?" Tom announced as he strode toward the gate. The women on the ground whirled to face him and gasped, then jumped together, effectively concealing the delivery boy's presence.

"Oh, no, not at all," Veronica said in a too-chipper voice. "We're just out for a little stroll."

"I suppose Mrs. Suddath is practicing for tomorrow's mountain climbing expedition," Jo offered as she came up beside Tom.

Three pair of eyes rounded in horror. "Mountain climbing?" they asked simultaneously.

"Look," the kid cut in. "I ain't got all night. Somebody's gotta pay for these two double cheese, double pepperoni, thick crust pizzas."

"Pizza? What pizza?" Sandra chirped from her position near the top of the fence.

Tom shoved a couple of bills through the fence. "Share it with your coworkers," he told him.

"Thanks, mister."

Tom glared at Beulah and Mildred. "You ladies have some explaining to do." They nodded eagerly. The car carrying the pizza spun onto the highway, no doubt reminding the ladies of their loss.

"Mr. Caldwell," Sandra summoned him humbly.

Tom lifted his irritated gaze to meet hers.

She smiled and batted her lashes flirtatiously. "I have a slight problem here."

Tom frowned. "What sort of problem?"

"I don't think I can get down."

EIGHT

At 1300 hours on Saturday afternoon all twelve ladies stood in formation awaiting instructions. Hands behind her back, Jo paced before the scraggly looking group. She favored each one with a severe glare as she passed. Today she wore her Army issue battle dress uniform and her combat boots. She wanted to leave no doubt in anyone's mind that she meant business.

Jo Passerella had had enough.

Jo had rousted the ladies from bed at 0530, and they had been making field-ready preparations since. Now, they stood prepared to depart. Each carried a bedroll, two water-filled canteens, and a knapsack stocked with a day's rations on their back. Jo had personally selected the proper attire from individual wardrobes for this little getaway. No one carried anything she had not authorized.

"Ladies, I am a firm believer in not giving up." Jo paused before the group and surveyed each repentant face. "Otherwise I might have walked out days ago. But the Army taught me something way

back in basic training: Never say die. And I promise you that before this weekend is over, all of you
will understand a great deal more about that
motto."

Nobody even blinked. Jo wondered vaguely if they
were catatonic or simply fear-stricken. "Before we
get started, are there any questions?"

Sandra Suddath's hand went up slowly. "Sergeant
Jo," she started contritely. "Will it help any if we
say we're sorry?"

Jo glared at her, then called, "Left face!" The
women whirled to their left, the effect something
like dominoes falling. Jo blew out a breath of frustration at their complete disharmony.

She could do this.

She would do this.

"Forward, march!" she commanded. Moving
about as fast as molasses, the ladies marched toward
the designated trail.

"Jo."

Jo turned to face Tom. He had been watching
from his office. He stood directly in front of her
now, all rumpled and sexy-looking. Jo clamped
down on her lower lip to prevent the smile of approval that wanted to curl her lips. He already
knew too much about how she felt. She wasn't
about to give him any more ammunition. This little trip into the wilderness was definitely a good
idea. She needed some time away from Tom. Time
to come to her senses. Time for him to come to
his.

"Come to see us off?" she inquired in a nonchalant tone.

Tom glanced at the women marching away. "Are you sure you'll be all right?"

"Positive," Jo answered succinctly. She adjusted her regulation cap. "I'm a professional soldier. I can do anything."

Tom smiled then, one of those insanely appealing smiles that took her breath away. "Oh yeah, I forgot that little detail," he teased.

Jo nodded toward the slowly disappearing group. "I guess I'd better catch up," she offered as she started to back away.

He nodded. "Be careful, Jo." Anxiety tightened his chiseled features. "We have things to talk about when you get back."

"Right." Jo did a quick about-face and double-timed in the direction of her sissy squad. But she had a gut feeling that she would never be able to move fast enough to outrun Tom Caldwell. He wasn't the kind of man who let things go easily. He was determined. *He* wouldn't say die easily. Jo broke into a dead run.

Maybe if she tried a little harder, played a little tougher, he would understand. Sergeant Jo Passerella couldn't possibly fall in love with him. She was already promised to Uncle Sam.

Dusk had descended by the time the haggard group got within a half mile of the camp site. Sandra, Beulah, and Mildred straggled way behind. Jo frowned. If the whole group didn't get a move on, there wouldn't be time to set up camp before dark.

Jo trotted down to the back of the line. "Get a move on, ladies, you're slowing the rest of us down. Setting up camp in the dark is no party."

Veronica trudged a little faster, Beulah on her heels. Sandra still sluggishly put one foot in front of the other. She wasn't about to be intimidated.

"Can't we take a break now, Sergeant Jo?" the big blonde asked. She stopped to adjust her sleeves and fuss with her poufy hair.

The kid gloves went off. Jo walked straight up to Sandra and got in her face. "Until we reach our destination, Mrs. Suddath, there are only two acceptable reasons for stopping." Jo ticked them off on her fingers. "You pass out or puke."

Sandra's eyes widened in disbelief, then narrowed in outrage. "Well," she huffed. She straightened her wilted collar and squared her shoulders. "Since I'm not prone to either, I suppose I'll carry on."

"After you," Jo suggested with a wave of her hand.

Sandra sniffed, lifted her chin defiantly and marched after her cohorts.

Jo followed. There was no telling what Sandra would say to her beloved husband regarding Jo's actions. Who knew if Jo would even have a military career after this fiasco? She could only do her best.

Fifteen minutes later they reached the campsite Tom had shown Jo on the map. The clearing was large with a couple of cold fire rings. Jo scanned the darkening sky. They didn't have much time. She sure didn't want the women stumbling around after dark.

Jo dropped her canteens, bedroll and knapsack. She surveyed the group and quickly sorted her teams. "Crystal, you, Betty and Mildred sweep the area for usable firewood. Don't go too far and watch for snakes. I want you back here before it gets completely dark."

"Yes, ma'am," Crystal exclaimed. She and the other two left their bedrolls and knapsacks and hurried to obey Jo's orders.

Jo didn't bother correcting that "ma'am." Though it was proper to address her as sergeant, Jo knew Crystal meant well. Jo turned to the others. If only that could be said for the rest of them, she mused.

"Beulah, you, Sandra and Veronica spread the bedrolls, knapsacks and canteens in a wide circle here." Jo pointed to the largest fire ring and quickly demonstrated her instructions.

"When are we going to eat, Sergeant Jo?" Veronica asked as she set to the task she had been assigned. "I'm about to starve to death."

"That depends on you, Veronica. When everyone has completed their assigned tasks, we'll eat together." Jo didn't miss the grumbling coming from Sandra and Beulah's direction. Jo quickly detailed the remaining women to necessary tasks, like inspecting the sleeping area to see that there were no ant hills, snake holes and the like. The fewer surprises, the better.

By the time night became a reality, Jo, with the

help of all the ladies, had a fire going more for light than for heat. While they consumed their rations, they discussed the sights they had seen on their way up the mountain. They had crossed a wide, shallow stream using rocks for stepping stones. Several types of birds had been spotted and identified. Even a family of deer had watched their progress curiously from a safe distance.

"Now I know why my husband never goes into the field anymore," Sandra groused as she scowled at her half-eaten field rations. "A person could waste away to nothing on this stuff."

"Actually," Crystal spoke up, "I think they're pretty good."

Sandra shot her an annoyed look. "You would."

"Actually," Jo clarified, "these rations were specially designed to provide the necessary nutrients to sustain life. Wasting away isn't a concern."

Sandra rolled her eyes and bit into her beef jerky. Jo smiled to herself. If she couldn't keep the ladies away from the food, she would take them where there was none. Except, Jo amended, the field rations they could carry. Jo had explained before they left that each person was in charge of their own rations of food and water. When they're gone, they're gone, she had told them. The women guarded their food and water with their lives. Sandra might complain about the cuisine, but it beat nothing. And there was absolutely nothing, excluding wildlife and a few berries, between here and Camp Serenity, a half day's walk away.

A coyote howled in the distance.

"What was that?" Veronica asked, wide eyed.

"A coyote," Jo replied offhandedly.

A dozen pair of eyes rounded. "Should we be worried?" Mildred asked what no one else would. "I mean, do they attack?"

Jo shook her head. "Not as long as we keep the fire going. They're afraid of the fire."

"Sergeant Jo?"

Jo turned to Crystal. "Yes."

"Do you wish that the general had assigned someone else to this job?"

All eyes were on Jo again. She thought for a moment before she answered. She thought of all she had been through with these women in the last few days and considered that they still had a whole week to go. Then Jo allowed the image of Tom to fill her mind. How could she regret knowing him? She couldn't.

Jo smiled. "No, ladies, I don't. I wouldn't have missed this mission for anything."

"But would you do it again?" Crystal pressed the issue. "I mean, if you were asked."

"Absolutely," Jo answered without having to think about it. And therein lay the problem. No matter how much she suffered in the future for this little adventure, personally and professionally . . . Jo wouldn't trade her time with Tom for anything in the world.

Jo awoke just as the sun peeked over the treetops. Gold and rust streaked across the morning sky. She stretched in her bedroll and admired nature's glory. She allowed herself a few peaceful moments of relaxation before rising. She thought of how it would feel to snuggle up with Tom on a morning like this. How his arms would feel around her, his lips on hers. Tom, the man with the big heart who loved kids and dogs. The man who now owned major property in her heart. Jo blinked away the too-vivid fantasy and sat up.

Those were things that took permanence and roots. Jo didn't have either. Couldn't have either in her chosen career. Sure, lots of soldiers were married, but it presented difficulties more often than not.

Jo frowned when she noticed Sandra asleep sitting up, a bundle of sticks and branches clutched in her arms. Coals that should have gone cold hours ago still glowed red in the fire ring. Jo's frown eased into a smile. Sandra had obviously kept the fire fed most of the night to keep the coyotes away.

Jo shook her head and got to her feet. Maybe she shouldn't have teased the women about the coyotes. Jo hoped Sandra had gotten at least some sleep last night. She would need it before this day was over. A twinge of sympathy niggled at Jo, but she quickly pushed it aside. She had to be tough. Sandra, more than the rest, desperately needed to learn the definition of self-discipline, and the importance of teamwork.

Jo's shoulders sagged when she considered how little self-discipline she had displayed where Tom was concerned. She blew out a disgusted breath.

Who was she to point fingers at anyone else? The general's words about this assignment being close to his heart still rang in Jo's ears.

She hurried into the cover of the surrounding woods to take care of personal business before she awakened the dozen sleeping beauties.

"Rise and shine, ladies, you're wasting daylight," Jo announced loudly when she returned.

Startled, Sandra jerked to attention. She looked around at the others, then quickly tossed her bundle of limbs next to the now cold fire ring. Once on her feet, she dusted her hands and gave Jo a feigned smile.

"Good morning, Sergeant Jo," she offered in her most sugary southern belle tone.

"Good morning, Sandra. I hope you slept well," Jo returned just as sweetly.

"I'll let you know as soon as I have my morning coffee," she replied with a smile and a rapid batting of her long false lashes.

Jo rocked back on her heels. She was going to enjoy this. "Unless you brought a magic wand with you in that knapsack, there won't be any coffee this morning." The whole week had been worth the look on Sandra's indignant face at that moment.

"However, there is a squeeze packet of orange juice included in your rations," Jo added with infinite pleasure. She knew her joy at the woman's expense was naughty, but she just couldn't help herself.

Sandra scowled. "God, I hate the wilderness," she muttered as she turned her back on Jo.

"Take care of any personal business, have your breakfast, and pack up. We leave in fifteen minutes," Jo informed the still-sleepy group.

The ladies grumbled and wandered around aimlessly for a couple of minutes, but before Jo had to remind them of the shortness of time, they were falling into a routine of sorts. Jo moved around the group, ensuring that everyone was properly prepared for the long walk ahead of them. She listened intently as she neared the troubling threesome that included Sandra, Mildred and Beulah.

"I'll give you fifty dollars," Sandra offered in a hushed whisper that was still loud enough for Jo to hear and understand.

"No way," Beulah muttered, shaking her head. "Mildred's already offered seventy-five."

Sandra gave Mildred an evil look. "Don't do anything you'll regret, Milly," she threatened.

Mildred returned her icy glare. "You say one word to Vince and I'll tell George about the ice cream."

Jo bit the inside of her cheek to keep from laughing out loud. She eased another step closer.

Sandra turned her determined attention back to Beulah. "A hundred and that's my final offer, Beulah. So don't try to gouge me for more."

"Sold." Beulah said as she exchanged lunch rations with Sandra.

Once Sandra had the lunch packet in her hands she quickly shoved it into her knapsack. "Thank you, Beulah," Sandra said in that honeyed tone of hers. "I'll remember your loyalty."

When Sandra had gathered her things and sauntered away, Beulah looked at Mildred and giggled as quietly as she could. "What a sucker," she hissed, then quickly looked left to right. "She could have had Crystal's brownie for free. Crystal's allergic to chocolate."

Mildred doubled over with the effort to hold back her laughter. "You'd better not tell Sandra you knew that," she choked out.

"Get your butts in gear, ladies," Jo barked, breaking up their little tête-à-tête.

"Yes, Sergeant Jo." Mildred scrambled to her feet and hustled after Sandra.

Beulah swiped her eyes and stood, still smirking over her little coup.

"Beulah." Jo leaned close to the strapping older woman. "If I find out you took that money from Sandra, I'll tell Colonel Jackson about Mr. Caldwell's stolen clothes. I'm sure he won't find it amusing."

"What clothes?" Beulah demanded, her gaze narrowed suspiciously.

Jo smiled her triumph. "The ones I found under your mattress."

Beulah's expression wilted. "Oh, all right," she griped. "I won't take her money." Beulah snatched up her knapsack, then grinned. "That boy's got the cutest rear end I believe I ever did see."

Flabbergasted, Jo watched Beulah stride away. No point in arguing with the truth, Jo decided. There were a great number of things about Tom Caldwell that were cute . . . gorgeous, in fact. Jo frowned. But she wasn't supposed to be thinking about him right now. Forcing Tom's naked image from her mind, Jo gathered up her own belongings and set to the task at hand.

She had all day in the middle of nowhere, with nothing but her wits to entertain twelve spoiled ladies. Nothing in all her military training had prepared her for this.

Jo surveyed the good-for-nothing group standing before her. Well, she'd manage them somehow. It was a perfectly beautiful day. The sun was shining, the birds were singing, and the forest around them was breathtaking.

At that precise moment the sky darkened and thunder boomed in the distance.

The downpour lasted just long enough to get everyone and everything good and wet. A great deal of the trail was now muddy and slippery. They were supposed to arrive back at Camp Serenity by 1400 hours, but Jo was pretty sure at this point that they wouldn't make it on time—if they made it at all.

Sandra Suddath and her friends were a pain in the tush under optimum circumstances, Jo knew. But wet and miserable, they were unbearable. Every step they took was accompanied by endless complaints. They were sore; they were tired; they were hungry. They needed a bathroom. They wanted to stop.

Jo wanted to stop.

"Break time, ladies," Jo called out to her grumpy troops—if you could call them that.

"It's about time," Beulah complained as she sat down on her bedroll. She began unlacing her shoes. "My dogs are killing me," she muttered.

"Don't take your shoes off, Beulah," Jo warned. "You'll never get them back on if you do."

Beulah groaned her acquiescence.

Jo scanned the others to make sure no one else had gotten that bright idea. "Drink some water, please. You don't want to get dehydrated." Jo took her own advice and took a long pull from her canteen.

"What are we going to do about food?" Veronica whined.

Jo resisted the urge to remind them that they'd had lunch just over an hour ago. "We'll be back at camp in plenty of time for dinner," she said instead. "Maybe Hattie will have whipped us up another of her delicious chocolate cakes," she added slyly.

A symphony of groans sounded at that suggestion.

Mildred stood and turned slowly around. "We're not lost, are we, Sergeant Jo? None of this looks familiar to me. I don't remember seeing any of this yesterday."

Jo felt like wringing Mildred's neck for that remark. Panic rumbled through the rest of them. "No, we're not lost. We're simply taking a different trail back down the mountain, that's all." The ladies weren't convinced. "I thought it would make things more interesting."

"I'm sure Sergeant Jo knows exactly where she's going," Crystal stated above the suspicious chatter.

"Oh, Crystal, I'll bet you were always the teacher's pet in school," Sandra complained churlishly.

Crystal braced her hands on her hips and glared at Sandra. "I was not!"

Sandra stood and matched her stance. "I am in no mood for your perkiness," Sandra snapped. Her face flushed a darker red as her irritation obviously mushroomed. "I am wet. I am muddy. My thighs are chafed. My feet are swollen and tender. And I'm damned hungry. So stop being so frigging optimistic!"

Jo scrubbed a hand over her face. She considered all that Sandra had said and decided that the woman had left out a few things like smeared makeup, a loose false eyelash, and mussed hair.

All hell broke loose then. The women were evenly divided, with half defending Crystal, and half taking up Sandra's cause. Well, Jo mused, this little outing had certainly proven effective in teaching self-discipline and teamwork.

"Ladies," Jo called loudly.

The battle continued, growing louder by the minute.

"*Ladies!*" Jo bellowed in her loudest, deepest drill sergeant's tone.

Dead silence fell over the group. They all froze in place. Only their gazes moved, seeking out Jo.

"When you've resolved your differences, you may catch up with me." Jo adjusted the straps of her knapsack. "Otherwise, I wish you good luck in finding your way back to camp." Jo turned sharply and marched away.

Several seconds of shocked disbelief passed before Jo heard the group scrambling down the trail after her. She shook her head in frustration. It would almost be funny if this mission weren't so important to Jo. She laughed softly. Who was she kidding? It was damned funny and she knew it. These gals could star in their own sitcom.

"Wait, Sergeant Jo, wait," Sandra wailed. "We're coming!"

Jo paused. She turned just in time to see Sandra start sliding down a particularly slippery incline. Jo sprinted toward her. Barely a second before Sandra went down, Jo was there, grabbing her arm and slowing her fall. When she had Sandra back on her feet, she breathed a sigh of relief. That was too close for comfort.

"I'm okay," Sandra assured her breathlessly.

Jo's heart was pounding so hard that she felt certain it would burst at any moment. "Good," she managed past the lump of pure fear lodged in her throat.

Sandra adjusted her clothing and started on down the trail. Jo waited to make sure each of the ladies made it past the slippery incline before starting after them. She blew out the breath she'd been holding. If Sandra or one of the others had been hurt, it would have been Jo's fault. The idea of one of them really suffering because of something she did was scary. Success wasn't worth one of them getting injured. Jo would just have to make sure that didn't happen. She double-timed it back to the front of the line. She intended to be the first to encounter any more risky areas. And this time she would be paying attention.

As Jo reached the front of the line and fell into a slower gait, the toe of her boot snagged on an exposed root. Before she could catch herself, she tumbled sideways and down the wooded slope to the right of the trail. Jo curled into a ball to protect herself as best she could. Moments later, a tree trunk stopped her rolling, tumbling journey.

Jo sat up and straightened her leg. The sharp stab of resulting pain wrenched a groan from her. Her shin had taken the brunt of the impact, and she'd twisted her ankle but good on the way down. She shrugged out of her gear and slowly struggled to her feet.

"Sergeant Jo! Are you all right?" someone shouted from up above her.

Jo looked up to find the disgusted dozen clambering down the slope in her direction, their panicked voices echoing through the woods.

"I'm okay," Jo said halfheartedly. She tested her weight on her injured ankle. A flash of pain knifed through the joint and then upward. No way in hell would she make the rest of the walk out of here. Nothing felt broken, but there was too big a chance that she might do worse damage. Jo swore under her breath.

Crystal was the first one to reach her. "Are you sure you're okay?" Her frantic gaze swept over Jo, then locked with hers. "Oh, God, you're not. I can see the pain in your eyes." Crystal's face paled.

Eleven more panicked faces looked at Jo, and all talked at once.

Jo held up her hands to quiet the senseless hysteria. "I'm okay, but I'm not going to be able to walk out of here."

Gasps punctuated her announcement.

Jo shook her head. She clenched her teeth for a moment until the fresh wave of pain subsided a bit. "It's not a big deal, ladies. You just follow the trail and it'll take you back to the camp. There's no way you can get lost. So don't panic."

"And what about you?" Beulah, elbowing her way to the front, demanded.

"You can send Mr. Caldwell and Reg back to get me. I'll be fine until they get here." *I'm sure as hell not going anywhere,* Jo didn't say.

More worried chatter bounced back and forth.

"I don't think it's a good idea," Veronica said with a shake of her head. "What if something happened to you before we could get help?"

Jo heaved a frustrated sigh. "Nothing is going to happen to me. I'm perfectly safe."

Sandra's eyes suddenly rounded in horror. "What if the men can't get back to you before dark? What about the coyotes? You don't have a fire!"

Somehow Jo had known that would come back to haunt her. "If you leave now, and *hurry*, they can be back here before dark," Jo said, effectively skirting the issue.

Crystal shook her head. "But we don't know how to tell them where you are." She shrugged nervously. "I don't know north from south."

Jo rubbed her eyes with the heels of her hands, then settled them firmly on her hips. "Look, just stay on the trail. Tell Tom I'm on the alternate trail. He'll know the one you mean. Tell him I'm about two hours walking distance west of Camp Serenity."

"Spread out, ladies," Sandra Suddath demanded as she shoved Beulah aside and came toe to toe with Jo. She glared down at Jo with lead in her gaze and her hands planted on her ample hips. "Sergeant Jo and I need a few minutes alone."

Nobody moved. "Now," Sandra bellowed.

Uncertain, but unprepared to defy the queen bee, the ladies scrambled back up the hillside.

Jo let go a weary breath and leveled her gaze on Sandra's. "Okay, Mrs. Suddath, what gives?"

"You know what you've got, Sergeant Passerella?"

"No, but I'm quite certain you're going to fill me in," Jo returned. This was it, the showdown. The general's wife was about to have her say, and most likely inform her of just what she intended to tattle about to her husband.

"Spunk and attitude." Sandra plopped down onto the ground directly across from Jo and blew out a tired breath. "That's why the general chose you for this assignment. He wanted to be sure my friends and I would not only be well taken care of but motivated into action. He knows how I can be." She smiled with true southern charm. "After all, we've been married for twenty-five years."

You could have knocked Jo over with a feather. "I appreciate you being straight with me."

Sandra sighed. "Oh, I know I've given you a hard time, but that's just me. It's nothing personal."

Jo grinned. "I never thought it was."

"It's not often that I meet my match," Sandra admitted with a slight nod of approval.

"It's not often," Jo countered, "that I'm challenged to utilize my full potential."

Sandra's gaze grew somber then. "The bottom line is this. I respect you, Sergeant Jo. You've worked hard for us. And if you think for one minute that we're going to walk out of here without you, then you're a card shy of a full deck." She stood. "So, suck it up, soldier, and let's be on our way."

"Sandra, I can't walk out of here." Jo gave her an imploring look she hoped would convey the truth in her words. "Trust me, if I could, I would."

Sandra shrugged one shoulder and made a dismissing face. "Who said anything about you walking?"

NINE

Tom looked at his watch for the dozenth time in the last hour. Jo and the ladies should have been back long before now. Something had to be wrong. If only he knew which trail they had taken, he would head out after them. But he had no way of knowing. Jo hadn't been sure which route they would return by. She wanted to make that decision based on several factors, she had said. Tom raked his fingers through his hair and dropped onto the porch steps outside his office. Maybe the rain had slowed them down, he reasoned. That had to be it.

"They're not back yet?"

Tom shook his head as Reg sat down next to him. Though he tried not to show it, Tom knew Reg was almost as worried a he was. The only difference was that Reg wasn't in love with Jo.

Tom definitely was.

Sometime between seeing them off yesterday afternoon and waking up this morning, Tom had realized that he had fallen for her, head over heels. He wasn't sure what it would take to make the little soldier his, but he intended to give it his best shot. None of his past relationships had ever come close to what he had with Jo. She was all he thought about anymore.

All he wanted.

All he needed.

"Should we be worried?" Reg asked, breaking into Tom's thoughts.

Tom shrugged. "I don't know, Reg." Tom had never been so torn in his life. He didn't want to make Jo look bad by going after them unnecessarily. But still, every moment they delayed was precious time. Once it was dark, their chances of finding them would diminish greatly.

"You, Hattie and I could split up and head out after them if you think we should," Reg suggested quietly. "It might be best not to wait much longer."

Reg had read his thoughts. Tom looked at his watch again. "We'll give them another half hour. If they're not back by five, we'll head out."

Reg sighed. "They're probably just enjoying the scenery."

"Maybe," Tom allowed optimistically, "but I doubt it. Chances are they're wet and muddy, and they're definitely out of food."

Reg lifted a skeptical brow. "I see your point."

Tom refused to consider that something might have happened to Jo. He frowned. Then again, even the best swimmer could drown. Jo might know how to handle herself, but accidents still happened.

Tom pushed up from the steps. "Maybe we'll go ahead and start now."

"I'll get Hattie," Reg offered, already up and heading toward the dining cabin.

The sound of Sandra Suddath's practiced southern belle tone was like music to Tom's ears. He turned toward the edge of the woods beyond the empty quadrangle. The chattering group of women emerged from the trees smiling and laughing as if they'd had the time of their lives. As they grew nearer Tom could see that they were indeed muddy and frazzled looking, but that didn't seem to have darkened their moods. He frowned when he didn't see Jo among those in front. His chest constricted with fear.

Several women started to wave and call hellos, and it was then Tom saw the thing that made his concerns a reality. Beulah, Veronica and a couple of the other ladies lugged a makeshift stretcher . . . carrying Jo.

"What the hell?" Tom blinked and looked again.

"Well, I'll be," Reg said, shaking his head in disbelief. "Who would have thought this group could pull together for anything?"

Tom rushed to Jo's side, worry dogging every step. "What happened?" he demanded hoarsely.

"It's not as bad as it looks," Jo assured him with a tremulous smile.

"Stand back, Mr. Caldwell," Beulah ordered. The ladies lowered Jo, on the bedrolls they had fastened together for a stretcher, to the ground.

Jo looked up and gave the ladies a wide smile. "Good job, ladies. I'm very proud of all of you."

Beulah and Veronica slapped a high five. Others

were hugging and crying tears of what appeared to be joy. Tom couldn't be sure what had happened on that mountain, but whatever it was, it had done these ladies a world of good. They had never looked this happy after a workout. And Jo, well, she was the most beautiful vision he'd ever laid eyes on.

He turned his full attention to Jo and crouched down next to her makeshift stretcher. "Are you all right?"

She reached for his hand. "I think it's just a bad sprain and a lot of bruising."

Tom wrapped his fingers around her small hand. His heart stumbled at the overwhelming protective feeling that squeezed his chest. The full impact of the past three hours of pacing hit him square in the gut. "Dammit, Jo, I've been worried sick."

The smile she flashed him did strange things to his insides. "We're back safe and sound. So how about helping me up," she suggested.

He nodded, not trusting himself to speak at the moment. Tom gingerly lifted Jo to her feet. She was as light as a feather. He slid one arm around her waist for support. "I could carry you," he offered.

Jo glanced at the group of ladies who were engrossed in retelling the day's events to a seemingly fascinated Reg. Even Hattie had come out to greet them.

"That might not be a good idea. These ladies don't miss anything."

Tom flicked a glance at the disheveled bunch, and then at Reg and Hattie. "I guess you're right.

But I want to get you inside so I can get a better look at that ankle."

Before Jo could respond, the sound of an approaching vehicle captured her attention. A U.S. Army hummer braked to a stop a few feet away. Tom wasn't expecting anyone from the post. He felt Jo stiffen in his arms.

To Tom's surprise, General Suddath emerged from the passenger side of the vehicle. As he approached, Jo pulled out of Tom's arms and came to attention. Tom glanced at the injured foot now planted firmly on the ground. He knew it had to hurt like hell.

"General Suddath, sir," Jo announced and performed a practiced salute.

The general returned her salute. "At ease, Sergeant."

A hush fell over the women who were still recounting their tales to Reg. Sandra smiled and waved coyly at her husband. The general braced his hands on his hips and surveyed the scene for a long, tense moment before returning his gaze to Jo.

"What's going on here, Sergeant?" He looked Jo up and down. "And where's your headgear?"

"We've just returned from bivouac, sir. We had a little trouble and I lost my headgear."

General Suddath glanced at his wife and the other ladies once more. His expression was disapproving, to say the least. "I'd say you had more than a little trouble, Sergeant."

Tom didn't like the way this was going. He saw Jo tremble and he instinctively knew it was motivated by the difficulty of standing. Jo Passerella wouldn't show any outward display of fear when faced with a mere general. She was too polished, too professional for that. It had to be the pain.

"Yes, sir," Jo agreed.

"Perhaps we should discuss this issue further back at my office, Sergeant."

"Of course, sir."

Fury rushed through Tom. No, by God, there would be no further discussion at this time. In one smooth, unexpected move, Tom swept Jo into his arms before she could take the first step.

"General, I'm afraid your discussion will have to wait. Sergeant Passerella is injured and I intend to do something about that right now."

"If that is the case," the general began, arresting Tom's departure, "If you can't handle a march without injuring yourself, Sergeant Passerella, perhaps I should dismiss you and assign someone else to this camp." The older man glanced first at Jo, then his belligerent gaze locked with Tom's. The general was not accustomed to having his orders challenged by anyone, military or civilian.

"Please, Tom," Jo murmured. "Don't make this worse than it already is."

Tom took one look at Jo's stricken face and knew he had made a mistake only a civilian would make. He shouldn't have interfered. He told her with his eyes how much he regretted his actions.

"Just one cotton-pickin' minute," Sandra Suddath bellowed as she stormed forward. She looked a sight, all mud-splattered and mussed, but she aimed a ferocious glare at the general that made even Tom squirm. "If Jo goes, I go," she announced. "And I will be one unhappy camper if I have to go home early."

"Sandra." The general glanced around uneasily, then settled his indulgent gaze on his beloved wife. "This is not the time nor the place to question my authority," he reprimanded her gently.

Sandra reached up and shook her finger in his face. "George Suddath, you get right back into that hummer and go home. You're on my turf here."

The general lifted one gray brow. "Well, if you feel that strongly about it—"

"I do," Sandra insisted firmly.

"Whatever you say, dear," General Suddath relented. He turned back to Jo. "Well, Sergeant, it appears I've grossly misjudged the situation." He nodded in silent approval. "Carry on, Sergeant Passerella."

"Thank you, sir," Jo returned.

The general leaned down and placed an affectionate kiss on his wife's muddy cheek. "I'll see you next Sunday, my dear."

Sandra batted her lashes at him, and one flopped as if it might fly off at any moment. "Bye, George," she called as he climbed back into the vehicle and disappeared through the gate.

Wearily, Jo rested her head against Tom's shoulder. Tom knew he had just been given her unspoken approval to take care of her. And he intended to do just that.

* * *

Jo tried not to consider what the general had in store for her. Had Sandra not stepped in, Jo would certainly be on her way back to the post right now. Jo wondered briefly at Sandra's about-face. Somehow the two of them had bonded during the past week. Jo let go a big breath. She had seen the respect in Sandra's eyes when they'd had that little one-on-one chat. Jo had realized that the other woman's southern belle graciousness could be turned on and off at will. She was just glad to be on Sandra's good side, for whatever reason.

"Here you go." Tom sat down on the bed next to Jo and offered her a glass of iced tea.

"Thank you." Jo accepted the refreshment, then sipped it while keeping her eyes carefully averted from Tom's. Maybe it would have been better if she had gone back to the post with the general. Tom wanted to talk about things that Jo would rather avoid. How could she make him understand that they had no future together? The pain in her ankle was nothing compared to what her heart stood to suffer if she let what had happened between them develop into something more. It just couldn't go any farther.

As if it hadn't gone too far already, Jo chastised herself.

Tom had removed her boots and propped her injured foot on a stack of plump pillows. He agreed with her assessment that nothing appeared broken, but that hadn't kept him from wanting to

rush her to the emergency room. Jo caught herself
before she sighed. Tom was tempting her with
something she knew better than to want. Jo relaxed more deeply into the pillows he had placed
behind her and reminded herself not to get used
to any of this. Everything about her stint at Camp
Serenity was temporary. General Suddath's unexpected visit today had done nothing but drive that
point home for Jo. She and Tom were from two
different worlds, with no place to meet in the middle.

Jo closed her eyes and pushed the memory of his
sweet lovemaking away. This was all temporary, she
reminded herself.

"Tell me what else I can do to make you feel
better," Tom offered softly.

Jo set her glass on the table next to her bed
and braced for the explosion of emotions meeting
his gaze would detonate. "There's nothing else
you can do, Tom," she said in as strong a voice
as she could marshal. Somehow she had to make
him understand that a relationship between them
would never work. Heat and desire rushed
through her veins when she looked into his eyes
at last.

He placed one hand on either side of her and
leaned closer. "You're sure about that?" His gaze
lingered on her lips, making Jo's heart pound in
spite of her determination not to react.

"Positive," she replied without conviction.

Those twinkling blue eyes searched her face. His

lips slid into a slow, knowing smile. "Did you know that you have the cutest freckles?"

Jo curbed her own smile. "Freckles are not cute, Tom," she argued. "They're a skin abnormality." He leaned closer still. Jo's breath caught.

Tom kissed the tip of her nose. He pressed his forehead to hers and sighed. "Tell me you don't feel this, Jo. Tell me and I'll pretend I don't." His warm breath whispered across her lips, sending a fresh wave of need through her. "I have to know."

Jo's hands went to his broad shoulders. The feel of hard male muscle beneath her palms made her ache for his touch. "Tom, it's not that simple. What you feel right now won't be enough."

He tilted his head, putting his lips temptingly close to hers. "We don't need to complicate the issue. Yes or no, that's all I need to hear."

Desire, electric and alive, made Jo clench her fists in his shirt. "Yes, damn it, yes. I feel it. The problem is, what are we going to do about it?"

Tom brushed a kiss across her lips, and the sweetness and tenderness of it shattered the last of Jo's defenses. How could she refuse this man? Whatever the future held for her, the one thing Jo wanted right now was to feel Tom's arms around her.

"Don't worry," he murmured between kisses that quickly turned hot and frantic. "We'll figure something out. I promise."

As Tom's lips closed over hers, Jo did something she had never done before in her entire military career: she put the future out of her mind and concentrated on the present.

On this moment with Tom.

Tom finally realized what it was he worried that he might miss. That one elusive thing that always seemed to escape him because he was so absorbed in his work. He had somehow instinctively known that without it, he would never be complete. Never be as happy or fulfilled as he could be. But he couldn't quite grasp what it was. He knew now.

Jo. Of course, he hadn't known her until two weeks ago. But she was that one thing that was missing in his life. She completed him. They had made love every night this past week. Sometimes at his cabin, sometimes at hers. Once even in the showers when everyone else was safely tucked in for the night. Desire welled inside Tom even now. Jo was everything he wanted, and all he would ever need. And he was about to lose her.

General Suddath had already informed Tom that another drill sergeant would be assigned to Camp Serenity during the final four-week session. Jo wouldn't say what had transpired during that one appearance she'd been commanded to make at the general's office. But Tom had a feeling that it hadn't been good, at least not for Jo. It was so damned unfair. He desperately wished she would confide in him.

But she wouldn't.

Jo was leaving.

And Tom's life would never be the same.

Tom watched without really seeing as the twelve retreat participants put on a fashion show, hosted by Reg, for their attentive spouses. All twelve women had shed at least five pounds. Each sported a fully accessorized ensemble as they paraded across the stage like newly discovered models. Tom had observed with astonishment the change in them during the past week, the leading example set by Sandra Suddath. No one complained. They all worked together and followed instructions. Reg had been so impressed with their newfound interest and cooperation that he had planned this fashion show as a reward. Even Hattie'd had a change of heart. The elderly cook had insisted on preparing a sit-down dinner for today's farewell festivities. Tom was absolutely amazed.

In just twenty-four hours twenty teenagers would fill the cabins outside. All would return to normal.

Except Tom's heart.

An announcement from Sandra Suddath jerked Tom from his brooding. Sandra motioned for Jo to come forward. Tom turned to the woman sitting beside him in her fancy military uniform. His chest tightened as she stood and slowly walked to the front of the room. Jo still limped a little, but that didn't stop her. Tom sat up straighter in his chair, his gaze glued to the woman in dress greens.

"Sergeant Jo," Sandra began, then paused to swipe at her tear-filled eyes. "We'll never be able to fully relate the way you've touched our lives. But the other ladies and I wanted to somehow show our appreciation to you for all that you've done."

"That's not necessary, Mrs. Suddath," Jo insisted, her voice wavering.

"Well, you know how the Army is," Sandra said with a wave of her hand, "we'll use any excuse to give someone a plaque."

Laughter rumbled through the dozen military officers in attendance. Even Tom smiled. Sandra was quite a character. Tom didn't miss Reg and even Hattie taking the occasional swipe at their own eyes.

Beulah stepped forward and passed a wood and brass plaque to Sandra. Sandra held the plaque at arm's length and recited the inscribed words.

"To Sergeant Jo Passerella," she read. "For dedication above and beyond the call of duty." She paused to compose herself, then cleared her throat and continued, "For your never-ending patience and caring attitude." Sandra lowered the plaque and turned to Jo. "And for never saying die when faced with the impossible." Sandra threw her arms around Jo and hugged her close.

General Suddath was the first to stand when the applause echoed through the room. The show of appreciation from the audience, as well as from the ladies who were taking turns hugging Jo, went on and on. Tom waited as patiently as he could while each of the officers thanked Jo, Reg, and Hattie. They all shook his hand too, but he barely paid attention. He just wanted to reach Jo.

It seemed like forever before the crowd started to

thin and move toward the dining room for Hattie's dinner. Finally Tom had Jo alone. He watched as she admired her plaque. He wondered if she were stalling. Who was he kidding? He knew she was stalling.

She wanted to slip out of his life as quickly and suddenly as she had dropped in. Temporary duty, that's all her time here had been.

Tom tucked his hands into his pockets and walked over to where Jo stood quite obviously ignoring him. "Mission accomplished, Sergeant Passerella."

Jo turned and gifted him with a watery smile. "So it would seem," she agreed. A definite hint of sadness tinged her voice.

Tom stared at the floor for a time, afraid to say what he wanted to say, yet even more afraid of not saying it. He lifted his gaze back to Jo's and knew now was the time. The next few minutes would affect the rest of his life as well as hers. Tom knew beyond all doubt that if he let her slip away from him without at least asking her to stay, he would always regret it.

"Jo—"

Jo shook her head, cutting him off. Her eyes were suspiciously bright. "Don't say it, Tom," she pleaded. "Anything we say now will only make it more difficult for both of us to do what we know we have to."

He struggled with the anxiety mounting inside him. No way could he just watch her walk out. "So you want to take the easy way out, is that it?"

She looked away. "That's right."

Tom wanted to shake her. Why couldn't she see that what they could have was worth whatever diffi-. culties they had to overcome? "You can just walk away and not look back?" He flung his arms in the air in frustration, then quickly crossed them over his chest to prevent himself from reaching out to her. "Nothing we shared this past week makes you want to think twice?"

His words had an impact this time. She trembled. Her own frustration and anger was clear when her gaze reconnected with his. She glared at him for two long beats before she spoke. Tom knew she was gathering her resolve. His was gone. Desperation had long since replaced it. A whirlwind of emotions churned inside him.

"What happens when I receive a new assignment and have to move across the country?" she demanded, her anger and frustration rising. "Or to another country altogether?" She set her plaque aside on a nearby table, braced her hands on her slender hips and moved in for the kill. "Are you going with me, Tom? Because when the orders come I sure as hell have to go."

Tom blinked. He wasn't prepared to think that far ahead. Not yet anyway. They needed to take this one step at a time. To build on what they had started. The rest would come in due time.

"Is that your answer?" she snapped. "What about when I'm assigned to some third world country where the political situation is volatile and family members aren't allowed? What then, Tom?"

She swallowed, hard. "Will you wait patiently stateside?"

"We need time to talk, to figure this out," he countered, defeat weighing heavy on his shoulders.

"Time won't change the way things are," she said wearily.

"I only know what I want." Tom wished there was some way he could make her understand just how much he cared for her.

Jo laughed softly. "But the price is too high for you, is that it?"

A muscle jerked in Tom's tense jaw. "I'm willing to compromise."

Jo shook her head and moistened her lips. She was very close to crying and that affected Tom beyond all reason. The last thing in the world he wanted to do was hurt her. He couldn't even bear the thought.

"You just don't get it," she maintained. "The price is everything, Tom. It's all or nothing. If your heart's not in it, then we have nothing to discuss."

"All right then," he said tautly. He didn't have too much pride to be the first to say the words. "I love you, Jo. I'll do whatever it takes. I'll leave Waynesville. I'll go wherever you go."

She stumbled back a step, then shook her head.

She didn't know. Tom almost staggered with the impact of that realization. Jo really hadn't known or even suspected, it seemed, that he loved her enough to sacrifice it all, that he was willing to give up everything. The shock, the disbelief, it was all right there in her big, brown eyes.

"I have to go." Jo brushed past him and ran from the room without looking back.

In shock himself, Tom watched her run away. How could she not have known that he loved her? He had shown her in every way he knew how.

But he hadn't told her until this minute.

He was either too late or Jo didn't feel the same way.

TEN

"At ease, Sergeant."

"Thank you, sir." Jo relaxed as much as possible, considering what was likely to happen. She had known after her last meeting with General Suddath that he was not pleased with the way Jo had handled his wife's two-week retreat at Camp Serenity. Choosing to be diplomatic, he had simply told her at that time that he intended to send in Sergeant Riggs to replace her. Jo had said "yes sir" and that had been the end of the meeting. What else could she say? He was her superior officer.

Obviously in the three days Jo had been back at the post, General Suddath had had time to reconsider his oversight of her less-than-acceptable performance of duty. Now would come the reprimand . . . or worse.

General Suddath paced the length of the room before he stopped and turned back to her. "Sergeant Passerella, I've given a great deal of thought to the time you spent at Camp Serenity. And it grieves me that I have allowed these past three days to pass without acting on my thoughts."

Jo swallowed tightly. Here it comes, she told herself and braced for the bad news.

The general retraced his steps. He rubbed his chin thoughtfully. "I've considered all that my wife has told me," he continued. "I've even given due regard to what the other ladies had to say about the goings on during that two-week period. It's a story I won't soon forget." He shook his gray head. "And I have to tell you, Sergeant, I'm more than a little disappointed—"

"Sir, I can explain," Jo said abruptly, then caught herself. Her eyes rounded in disbelief. She had just interrupted the general. Damn! What was wrong with her? Her broken heart was obviously affecting her brain.

One gray brow arched in question. "May I continue, Sergeant?"

Jo moistened her lips. "Of course, sir."

He squared his shoulders and clasped his hands behind his back. His solemn gaze settled on hers. "As I was saying, Sergeant . . . I am sorely disappointed in the behavior of my wife and her friends. I cannot—"

Jo jerked her head in his direction. "I beg your pardon, sir?"

The general frowned. "Sergeant Passerella, has your hearing been impaired?"

Jo took a deep, calming breath. "No, sir. I'm sorry, please continue."

He glared at her. "Thank you, Sergeant." He

cleared his throat. "When Mrs. Suddath related the details of their shenanigans, I believe she called them, I was appalled. Grown women behaving like children." He directed his disturbed gaze at Jo. "I'm surprised you didn't report their behavior immediately, Sergeant."

Jo considered her response. Maybe she did have a hearing problem. Was the general, in some roundabout way, trying to let her off the hook? No way! Jo resisted the urge to shake her head. That couldn't be right. She was clearly delusional.

"Well, sir," she began when he shifted impatiently. "I considered the assignment a challenge." *Yeah, right,* Jo scoffed silently.

"Whatever the case, Sergeant," he replied dismissively, "I would like to personally commend your handling of the situation. You did a fine job considering the circumstances and I'm most grateful."

Huh? Jo looked quickly from side to side. When would someone jump out and say, "Surprise, you're on Candid Camera!"

Jo took the general's continued silence as her cue. "Thank you, sir. If that's all, sir, I'll report back to my troops."

General Suddath thoughtfully stroked his chin a moment. "Actually, Sergeant, there is one other thing we need to discuss."

Jo did a mental double take. Uh-oh. She knew this was too good to be true. Now came the kicker. She held her breath.

"I've been giving some thought to my hasty decision of removing you from the Camp Serenity assignment."

Jo's breath rushed out of her lungs. Boy, he'd been doing an awful lot of thinking lately where she was concerned.

"Considering your patience and ability to see the best in people, I believe you would be a true asset to the camp. So, I've decided to send you back."

Jo's head shook before her brain could give it the command not to.

"You have a problem with that, Sergeant?"

"No, sir," she said immediately, and swallowed. "Yes, sir," she amended cautiously. "I think I would best serve this command right here on the post."

The general cocked his head and studied her. "Are you saying, Sergeant Passerella, that you know what serves this command better than I?"

"Oh, no, sir," Jo exclaimed. She was getting in deeper all the time. Did they court-martial soldiers for stupidity? The image of Tom's amazing blue eyes kept appearing before her eyes, distracting her. The memory of his kisses, his lovemaking was playing havoc with her ability to reason.

"I'm just . . ." Jo didn't know what to say.

"Confused?" the general offered.

She nodded. "Yes, sir." How did he know?

"Welcome to the club, Sergeant." A small smile got past his authoritative demeanor. "Love does that to you, so you'd might as well get used to it."

"I don't understand, sir," Jo said, more than a little bewildered. She couldn't have heard him right. She was going deaf *and* getting stupid.

The general sighed. "What's to understand, Sergeant? I've given an order, you obey."

Jo opened her mouth to speak but he halted her with one upraised palm.

"I would consider it a personal favor, Sergeant."

Confusion reigned supreme. "A favor, sir?"

"My wife has threatened to kick me out of the house if I don't send you back to Mr. Caldwell ASAP," he finally said with defeat.

"To Tom?" Jo frowned. How could the general know? "But why?"

"Sandra seems to think you're in love with the man, Sergeant." The general looked disgruntled. "Are you suggesting my wife is wrong?"

Jo struggled with the response her mind wanted to make versus the one her heart shouted loudly. "No, sir," she said finally.

"Well then." General Suddath smiled. "Fall out, Sergeant Passerella. Your assignment begins immediately."

"Yes, sir. Thank you, sir."

Jo walked out of the general's office totally and utterly confused. How could Sandra have known? Jo and Tom had been so careful. She shook her head. Hell, it was probably written all over both their faces.

When Tom had abruptly announced that he loved her, Jo had been confused . . . scared. Was he just buying time? Did he mean it? How could she know? In the three days that had passed, Jo'd had time to think. If there was any chance Tom loved her, she should go for it. Shouldn't she?

Love didn't come along every day. Tom's words echoed through her mind . . . *something you might wish for the rest of your life you hadn't let slip away.*

But would Tom still want her after she'd walked away from him like that?

"Sergeant Passerella," Specialist Curry interrupted Jo's troubling thoughts. "The general instructed that I drive you out to Camp Serenity whenever you're ready to go."

Jo turned to the general's driver. "Thank you, Specialist." She chewed her lower lip, then asked, "By the way, do you know of a pet store or a pound in the area where I could get a dog?"

Curry shrugged. "The Humane Society always has dogs to adopt," he suggested.

Jo smiled. "Good idea, Specialist. How about taking me there first?"

Tom rifled through the sheaf of papers in his hand, then tossed the whole lot aside. He just couldn't concentrate. He forced thoughts of Jo away. He would not go down that road again. It was pointless. Her position was clear. She didn't love him as much as she loved her career. Tom raked his fingers through his hair and forced his attention back on the mountain of papers on his desk. So maybe he had been a fool for not saying the words sooner, but he had said them. Why wasn't that enough?

"I don't know why you don't just go get the woman."

Tom looked up to find Reg loitering in his door. "Go away, Reg," he said curtly.

Reg shook his head and made that annoying tsking sound. "You've got it bad, my friend."

Just what Tom needed. A love life analysis in the middle of the afternoon. Why didn't the man just turn the television on to Montel Williams and put in his two cents where it wouldn't hurt?

"Is there something you need, Reg?"

Reg strutted across the room. He folded one arm over his middle and rested his other elbow on it so that he could tap his chin. Tom swore silently. This was going to be a long one.

"Team four has a problem with attitude," Reg said finally, irritably. He shot Tom a look. "And if you say it has anything to do with my wardrobe, I'll scream. I swear I will," Reg threatened.

Tom blew out a breath and scrubbed a hand over his face. "Have Sergeant Riggs give team four a little extra training. That ought to take some of the wind out of their sails." Tom didn't really like Riggs, but he was a good PT coach—or at least he had been so far. Tom had a feeling he wouldn't have much liked anyone the General Suddath sent to replace Jo. Tom swallowed the regret that rose in his throat.

"I can't tell Sergeant Riggs anything. He's conspicuously missing this afternoon," Reg stated impatiently.

"Missing?" Tom frowned. "He was here at lunch."

Reg feigned a tolerant smile. "Well, be that as it may, he isn't here now."

Dammit. This was not a good sign. When a member of staff turned up missing, it usually meant—

"Tom! Reg!" Hattie skidded to a halt at Tom's door. "Come quick! Team four's hog-tied that new know-it-all sergeant and got him hanging from a tree!"

Tom groaned, then bounded out the door, across the porch and down the steps. This was all he needed. Reg followed right on his heels.

"Oh . . . my . . . God," Reg muttered as he came to an abrupt halt in the middle of the quadrangle.

Tom pulled up short when he caught sight of his new drill sergeant. Tom blew out a breath and shook his head. Sergeant Riggs, bound and gagged, was hanging like a baby in a makeshift cradle from a tree on the other side of the dining cabin. A four-letter word hissed past Tom's lips. This was going to be a difficult session if it started off this way.

Reg turned to Tom. "I suppose we should cut him down."

Tom shook his head again. "Yeah, I guess we should."

The sound of a vehicle approaching from the gate snagged Tom's attention. He turned around to find a U.S. Army vehicle braking to a stop in front of his office. The driver waved and then drove away, leaving a cloud of dust in his wake.

What the hell was that all about? he wondered vaguely. The raucous jeers coming from the group of teenagers gathered around Sergeant Riggs drew Tom's attention back in that direction. Before Tom turned away, he caught a glimpse of a silhouette in the settling dust. He jerked back around. His heart hammered against his sternum. It couldn't be, he told himself.

When the dust cleared, Jo stood staring back at Tom. A smile slid across Tom's face. She was back. He frowned when he realized that what he had thought was her duffel bag at her feet wasn't.

It was a dog.

An immense black Labrador wearing a big blue bow around his neck.

Reg slapped Tom on the back. "Go get her, lover. I'll rescue Riggs."

Tom walked slowly to where Jo waited. The dog wagged his tail enthusiastically.

"Jo," Tom offered by way of a greeting. She looked beautiful, uniform and all. It was all he could do to prevent himself from sweeping her into his arms and kissing her senseless.

"Tom," she returned. Her brown eyes were watchful, her expression guarded.

"It's good to see you." Tom knew he sounded wistful, as if it had been a lifetime since he had seen her instead of a mere three days.

She smiled, just a little. "It's good to see you, too."

Tom nodded. "Good," he said lamely.

Jo moistened those lips he so wanted to kiss. "I've come to relieve Sergeant Riggs."

Tom gestured at the commotion behind him, but he couldn't take his eyes off Jo. "Not a minute too soon, it would seem."

Jo leaned to the right to survey the scene and the

plight of the unfortunate Sergeant Riggs. "Looks that way," Jo agreed.

"Reg is working on getting him down," Tom assured her. He glanced over his shoulder and did a double take. Team four was busily stringing Reg up next to Riggs. Tom swore. He turned back to Jo. Why was she here? he wanted to ask. Even more, he wanted to take her in his arms and convince her that she was wrong, they could have a future together.

He nodded toward the rowdy kids. "I should help Reg."

Jo nodded. "That might be a good idea."

Tom started to go, but paused. "Why did you come back, Jo?"

She shrugged one shoulder. "The general ordered me to," she told him. "But that's only part of the reason."

Tom felt his hopes rising. He tried to slow the ascent, but he couldn't. He planted his hands at his waist and gave her a long, assessing look. "Yeah?"

Another of those tiny smiles teased her lips. "Yeah," she reiterated.

Tom ignored Reg's heated shouts. Hattie's booming voice echoed next. Tom had a bad feeling about that, but it could wait just one more minute. "What's the rest of the reason?" He had to know.

Jo extended her hand, offering Tom the dog's leash. "I brought you a present."

Tom glanced hopefully at the dog. "What's his name?"

Jo shot a nervous look at the dog, then back at Tom. "Blackie," she answered quickly.

Tom nodded. "Very original."

"I thought so." Her smile widened a little this time.

He accepted the leash. "Well, thanks, Jo. Being between dogs is no fun. But the bow will have to go."

"Absolutely." Jo took a big breath. "Well, are those my new trainees?" she asked, pointing toward the group of boys currently tying up Hattie.

Tom scanned the escalating chaos. "That's team four. We have three others just like them."

"Looks like a challenge."

"Yeah." Tom spoke calmly in spite of the fact that his blood pressure had to be at stroke level. He wanted to shake her; to demand to know the real reason she was here.

Jo adjusted her cap and beamed Tom a battle-ready look. "If you'll see to Blackie, I'll just mosey on over there and kick some adolescent ass."

Tom took a step back and waved a dismissive hand. "By all means, Sergeant Passerella."

Jo took three steps and paused. She twisted at the waist and looked back at Tom. "By the way, Caldwell, I'm in love with you and I expect you to back up every single one of those promises you made."

She talked tough, but Tom saw the hesitancy in her eyes. Tom crouched next to Blackie and stroked his back. "You can count on me, Jo."

Jo nodded, apparently satisfied. She turned and

took three more long strides before Tom stopped her.

"Jo!" Tom released Blackie and sprinted after her.

When she turned around this time, he grabbed her and kissed her until they were both gasping for breath.

"I love you, Jo." He smiled at the dazed look in her eyes. "We'll make it work."

Jo smiled. "Of course we will."

Blackie barked furiously.

"Will you two get on with it!" Reg shouted crossly.

"We really should—" Jo began.

"Yeah, I know," Tom agreed, but didn't release her. "We will, right after this." He kissed Jo again. And then again after that. . . .

ABOUT THE AUTHOR

At the age of nine Debra began writing stories for the characters who lived in her too-vivid imagination. By eighteen she had turned wife, mother, and career woman, leaving her writing behind. But those imaginary characters just wouldn't go away. For the next eighteen years while she did everything from managing a Captain D's to holding an executive secretarial position at NASA, the stories and characters continued to traipse around inside her head. Eventually they just had to come out, and Debra began the journey that would take her to where her heart had been all along—writing romance.

Write Debra with your comments at P.O. Box 64, Huntland, Tennessee, 37345.